THE WH

Viviane Moore was bo Her father was an architect and her mother a stained-glass artist. At nineteen she became a photographer and worked as a journalist for Paris Match press group. Her main area of interest has always been the Middle Ages and for some time she has devoted herself full time to writing her novels featuring the Chevalier Galeran de Lesneven. She lives in La Rochelle in France.

The White Path is the fourth 'Galeran' mystery.

ALSO BY VIVIANE MOORE

Blue Blood
A Black Romance
The Darkest Red

THE
WHITE PATH

Viviane Moore

Translated by
Adriana Hunter

ORION

First published in Great Britain in 2002 by Orion,
an imprint of the Orion Publishing Group Ltd.

A CIP catalogue record for this book
is available from the British Library.

ISBN 0 575 07327 6

Typeset in Stone Serif by
Deltatype Ltd, Birkenhead, Merseyside

Printed in Great Britain by
Clays Ltd, St Ives plc

The Orion Publishing Group Ltd
Orion House
5 Upper Saint Martin's Lane
London WC2H 9EA

THE WHITE PATH

The
White Path
of Saint-Jacques
in the
12th Century

Western Ocean

Bay of

LÉON
BR

Cordillera Cantabrica

Santiago
de Compostela

ASTURIAS

CASTILE

Montañas de León

León

Notre-Dame de Finibus-Terrae

Astorga

LEÓN

Sahagun

Burgos

Duero

Peter McClure

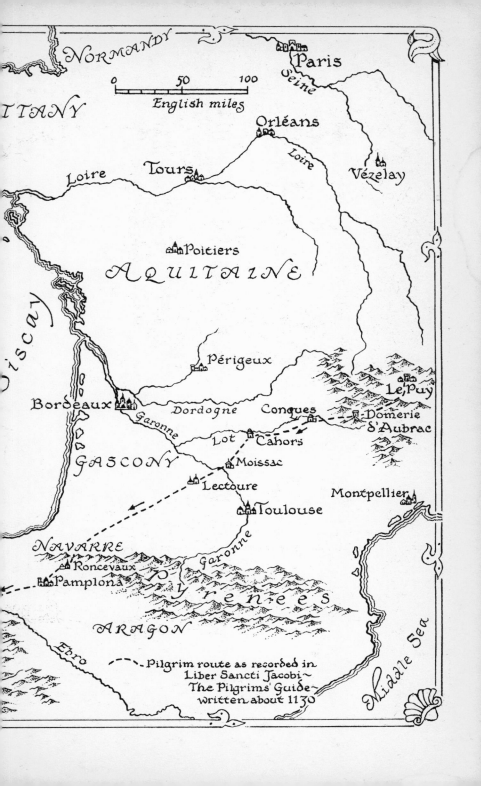

NORMANDY

Paris

Seine

0 50 100
English miles

TTANY

Orléans

Loire

Tours

Vézelay

Loire

Poitiers

A Q U I T A I N E

Périgeux

Le Puy

Bordeaux

Dordogne

Conques

Domerie
d'Aubrac

iscay

Garonne

Lot

Cahors

Moissac

Lectoure

Montpellier

GASCONY

Toulouse

NAVARRE

Garonne

Roncevaux

Pamplona

P Y R E N E E S

ARAGON

Ebro

— — — Pilgrim route as recorded in
Liber Sancti Jacobi ~
The Pilgrims' Guide~
written about 1130

Middle Sea

Translator's Note

The white path featured in this book is the route trodden by pilgrims since the ninth century to the tomb of the apostle Saint James. Saint James is known in French as *Saint Jacques*, and it is his French name that I have used in this translation because it is so intimately linked with the pilgrims themselves: they are called *Jacquets* and they wear scallop shells – *coquilles Saint-Jacques* – stitched to their coats when they have completed the pilgrimage.

Prologue

For some time now Galeran de Lesneven had felt that he was being followed. He forged on down the deserted little street and the rustling sound drew closer. Behind him something crept stealthily along the walls, its soft footsteps barely audible on the frozen snow.

When he turned round there she was, motionless, leaning against a crumbling section of wall. He raised his torch the better to see her. She was old, very old and wrapped in a shapeless, stained mantle.

The chevalier walked back towards her and his torch lit her face: she was a woman of the desert, a Moor, with prominent cheekbones and dark eyes ringed with kohl.

'What do you want from me, woman?' asked Geleran. 'Why are you following me?'

The old woman gave no reply. She just took his hand and held it in her bony fingers; then she shuffled right up to him so that they nearly touched, and her hawk-like eyes bore into him. At last, still silent, she raised a trembling index finger to the long scar which ran down the chevalier's forehead.

'It is you! This is how I saw you!' she muttered hoarsely.

'Where have we met before? Here in Vézelay? And, besides, where are you from?'

'I said that I had seen you, not that you had seen me,' retorted the woman, and for a moment a snarl distorted her toothless mouth. 'As for where I am from, it could be distant Damascus

3

. . . or Egypt, I no longer know . . . I am so old and I have lived so many lives, such long and cruel lives.'

'When did you last eat?' said the chevalier, seeing her shiver under her ragged clothes. 'You're in no fit state to be out on such a cold night. I shall take you to a tavern and they will serve you bread and gruel—'

'You take me for a pauper then!' cried the old woman, drawing her frail body up to its full height. 'I am the daughter of a king and in need of nothing.'

Galeran withdrew his hand sharply.

'I must leave you then.'

'Listen to me!' she almost shouted, clutching him with surprising force. 'Listen to me! I saw you, I tell you. You were walking on a white path and the stars in the sky were blotted with blood . . . There were young men coming towards you and when you reached out to touch them they died, and you could do nothing to save them.'

'What are you saying, woman, what are you talking about?' muttered the chevalier, tearing himself away from her.

The old woman's eyes rolled upwards in their sockets and she went on in a shrill voice which no longer seemed to belong to her, 'Death is close at hand. I see a man of your lineage. He is in great danger . . .'

Hearing these words, the chevalier's face darkened.

The old woman said breathlessly, 'Your enemy is there, walking beside you . . . he raises his arm and strikes . . . he thirsts for human blood! Oh, so much blood!' The woman seemed to come back to herself with a start. Despite the cold, she was streaming with acrid sweat. She stepped back, wiping her forehead hesitantly. 'You must be careful, Chevalier. Be careful . . . A pathway of stars covered in blood, remember that!'

Her voice faded gradually and, suddenly, he could no longer

4

see her. He was alone once more in the snow which had just started to fall again in great abundance.

PART ONE

E ultriea,
E sus eia,
Deus aia nos!

(And furthermore, and what is more, God gives us
succour!)

Marching hymn

1

The mountains had given way to more mountains, the rivers to torrents, and still they walked with the snow halfway up their hose. Then the old man raised his hand for them to stop.

The two women halted instantly, and Bruna wondered what might have caught the old man's attention. She strained her ears, and was relieved to hear the muffled calling of a bell; they were approaching some form of habitation, perhaps even, she hoped, the City of the Virgin.

It was now more than a week since they had left the Falgoux valley to travel to Le Puy Sainte-Marie. More than ten days of braving the icy cold of that month of March 1146 so as not to miss the Easter Mass and the pilgrimage to Santiago de Compostela. Their guide, an old shepherd from the estate, had led them along the ridges, carefully avoiding the routes where bands of ruthless armed men were rife. At night they had slept in little shepherd's huts abandoned by the mountain folk through the cold months of winter.

They had finally reached the fortified town of Saint-Flour, and the shepherd had agreed to their stopping at the monastery's hostelry so they could gather their strength after the testing journey through the mountains. Then they had set off again and crossed the gorges of the Allier. The old man knew the way to Le Puy Sainte-Marie, and knew how to cross the tumultuous waters at the Lavoûte-Chilhac bridge. Bruna paid for their passage and, after one last stop-off in an isolated barn, they had set out once more, taking care to stick to the recognised paths.

Not for one moment, during those long days of walking, had the snow stopped falling. Everything was so white that Bruna had lost all notion of time and no longer really knew where she was.

On that particular morning, the blizzard finally abated and a feeble ray of sunlight filtered through the leaden clouds. From the height of the sun, Bruna thought that it must be not far off time for the Sexte Mass, and she felt hunger gripping her insides. The old man had driven them on relentlessly and they had barely eaten anything but bread and cheese, even avoiding lighting a fire so as not to attract unwanted attention.

2

The shepherd stepped forward and, dropping their bags to the ground, held his great iron crook out towards three distant rocky peaks circled with cloud.

'Le Puy Sainte-Marie,' he said in the guttural patois of his mountain region. 'You are only a league away. Adieu, ladies, may the Lord watch over you!'

'But are you leaving us?' Bruna exclaimed with indignation as he turned on his heel. 'But what if it is not Le Puy?'

The man turned round, a stubborn expression on his lined face.

'Ah, but I know it is the City of the Virgin. May She protect you, Bruna the Untamed, and the woman with you. I will not go there, I shall return home,' he replied.

Bruna did not insist, she knew that once his mind was made up it was firmer than the rocks of Angouran. She watched him until he disappeared behind a curtain of trees. Her heart felt a little heavy. He was their last link with home, from now on they were alone.

'How strange,' she thought, 'it is a good ten days since we left our land and our bell towers, and I feel as if I belong nowhere. I am like a peregrine, a lonely wanderer, already. Now it is I who must lead my mistress to far-off Galicia. I, Bruna the Untamed. I who have only ever known our valley and the sky above it.'

Bruna had that particular kind of beauty that belonged to the mountains where, in times past, a troop of Huns had settled and founded their line. Her golden skin, her long shiny black hair, her almond eyes, her serious face which lit up with almost childish glee when she smiled, all betrayed her Mongolian origins.

She was as agile as a young goat and hard-working; it took a great deal to intimidate the Untamed. She tightened her grip on her great stick and bent to pick up the leather travelling bags, which she slung over her shoulder. Then she glanced sideways at her silent companion who had not moved, huddled in her mantle, her face hidden by a sort of black mantilla under her deep hood.

'Is she even there?' Bruna sighed, putting her hand gently on the woman's shoulder.

They set off again, crunching the snow under their boots. As they did, the first mists began to disperse and the Untamed stopped in amazement. What had been shapeless forms in the fog now made up the biggest city she had ever seen.

'Praise God, is it not beautiful and is not the world vast? Look, my lady!' cried Bruna, turning to her companion who seemed to have noticed nothing.

There it stood, dominating the plain and the surrounding woods, guarded by rocky peaks as sharp as wolves' teeth: the City of the Virgin. It lay at the foot of its great cathedral, built on a plateau of rock. The roofs were white with snow, and brightly

11

coloured banners fluttered above its ramparts.

A ray of sunlight picked out the shimmering dome of Notre-Dame, and Bruna interpreted this unexpected flash of dazzling light as a good omen. They had reached their first goal safe and sound and, God willing, would continue all the way to Compostela, the place that her master had described to her.

3

As the time for High Mass approached, despite the appalling weather, the roadways crowded with people, and the two women were carried along by the constant streams of pilgrims, traders, tumblers and peasants heading towards the fortified city wall. The closer they came, the greater the impetus of the crowd. Troubadours, with their characteristic hurdy-gurdies and rebecs, accompanied them on their way. Le Puy was famous for its poetic tournaments, and many were the *trouveurs* who vied with each other to carry off the live sparrowhawk, the symbol of supremacy.

There were not merely simple folk in the crowd, and Bruna watched in awe as high-born people rode past on their prancing horses. Dazed by the ringing of bells, the shouting, the whinnying of chargers and the barking of dogs, she gripped her companion's arm firmly as she drank in all the sights of this new world. She had never seen so much finery. The knights' surcoats were lined with ermine and silver squirrel, the palfreys wore cloaks of spun gold and silver, and even the townspeople had garments lined with fur, and not just cat fur or sheepskin, the girl was sure.

When they reached the gates of the city, she saw that they

were as black as the mouth of hell, taller than the tallest oak tree in Falgoux and studded like a paladin's doublet. Heaved and pushed in all directions, the two women finally found themselves inside the city walls, being jostled towards the Place du Plot where the crowd had gathered in front of the pillories.

Bruna had heard tell of these great wheels used to tie up thieves, putting them at the mercy of the vindictive townsfolk, but she had never seen one. Where she came from there were no thieves, for the simple reason that there was nothing to steal.

A detachment of armed men arrived and tied a man to the wooden structure. At first, the wrongdoer struggled and shouted, then he fell silent and stood motionless under the torrent of abuse and accusation from the crowd. On a sign from the sergeant, the men-at-arms slipped away, leaving just one orderly to watch over the unfortunate man.

Bruna clenched her fists anxiously and put her hand on the handle of her knife, wondering what would happen next. The gaping onlookers moved in slowly, forming a wide circle around the pillory. A young boy stepped forward and threw a rotten egg at the man's outstretched body. A townsman came over, scattering the children with one swish of his sleeve, and spat a long stream of saliva over the thief's face. The man tensed, straining against his chains but not daring to curse his torturers. The women encouraged their menfolk, shouting and waving their arms. Makeshift missiles flew through the air. Laughter spread. The orderly intervened only when a boy went to pick up a large stone.

'But what did he do?' Bruna asked the man next to her who was laughing so hard she was afraid he would burst his doublet.

'Fie, fie, what do I know, my pretty? He must have stolen something from someone. The last one we had was thanks to me, I caught him stealing meat from my stall.'

'But why is he not just given a proper punishment?'

The man stared at her as if the question were incomprehensibly stupid, and then turned away without even replying.

Bruna thought that where she came from it would not be done like this. The man would have been whipped and hounded out of the village. It was the act of humiliation itself which seemed to give these townspeople pleasure, a pleasure she could not grasp. The whoops of joy and the laughter grew louder, and Bruna looked away, already missing her mountains.

She felt stifled and realised that this town, which looked so beautiful seen from afar, was in fact dark and winding with its buildings huddled close together, and the filthy trampled snow underfoot . . . even the sky suddenly seemed narrow, as if held captive by the walls and roofs.

Not far from the pillory some traders had opened up their trestles. There were stalls in every direction, covered with brightly coloured spices, mantles, pastries, jewellery, shimmering fabrics . . .

The crowd suddenly surged back rapidly to let past a small mounted company heading for the cathedral. There was so much jostling and elbowing on the square that Bruna nearly lost sight of her companion. She only just caught her by her mantle in time and led her under a porch.

Bruna was out of breath. She needed to think: she was troubled and confused by so many people. She must find the Saint-Jacques hostelry in the rue de Rochetaillade quickly. It was there that Lord d'Apchon had booked board and lodging for them.

Leaning up against a wall dripping with melted snow was a young man who had been watching the two women for some time. He was poorly dressed, but his clothes were clean and he looked a fine enough man. He eventually made up his mind and went and stood full square in front of Bruna with these simple words, 'Good day to you, damsel, do you need a guide? I am hungry. Perhaps we can trade?'

Bruna looked over the young man's bony frame and decided he had an honest eye.

'Why yes. Have you been watching me long? Is it so obvious that we are not from these parts?'

'Indeed yes,' said the man with a wide smile. 'And that is by way of being a compliment, damsel.'

Bruna smiled for the first time since she had set foot in the town. 'Very well. Done! I'll buy you a bit of bread if you can take us to our inn in the rue Rochetaillade.'

The young man slapped his hand onto her outstretched palm.

'Come, it's up this way. If we go up here we'll get to the rue des Saulniers. That's not far from your street,' he said, slipping into a side street so narrow that Bruna had not even noticed it.

The passage was hemmed in by blind walls, and it must hardly ever have seen the sun. The air there was as cold as the depths of a cave and as fetid as a slurry pit. Bruna hesitated briefly before taking her knife out from under her cape and sidling along the walls that trickled with moisture. Her companion followed on behind her. The man waited for her, a mocking smile playing on his lips.

'You've no need of that with me, my girl,' he said, indicating the knife. 'Hide it. Even if I'm not from your region, I can be trusted.'

The young woman nodded and put the knife back in its case.

'Go on. We're right behind you,' she said gruffly.

The roads were steep in that part of town and the rue Rochetaillade was sloping and slippery like a pasture of spring grass. The man showed her a building with thick walls and an oak door. Above it hung a chunky wooden sign with a scallop shell, the emblem of Saint Jacques, carved upon it.

'There it is.'

Bruna looked at the place apprehensively. Everything in this town looked like a trap.

'What's it like there?' she asked. 'Will it be suitable for us?'

The young man glanced her over quickly.

'Keep hold of your knife, don't trust anyone and it'll be suitable for you. There is no better place to eat. As for her,' he said tilting his chin towards the silent, motionless woman next to them, 'I dunno. Is she a simpleton?'

'Indeed not! She is my mistress.'

'Ye' don't seem to have any need of a master, though,' retorted the man cheekily. 'Where are you from, girl?'

'Beyond Saint-Flour, in the foothills of the Auvergne,' replied Bruna.

'It's a long way and it's hard going in those parts,' the young man said seriously. 'It's hard here, too, but it's not the same. Have to watch out here. People aren't as honest as they are where you come from, and you don't always see them coming.'

'I understand,' said Bruna. 'Listen, I'll put my lady here in her room and then perhaps you could take me to the cathedral. If you'll wait for me, I'll buy you a bit of *fourme* to put on your crust.'

'Well, well, I'll wait for sure,' he replied with a delighted grin. 'It's a fair while now since I've eaten bread and cheese at the same time!'

The young woman from the mountains smiled and, taking her companion's hand, opened the tavern door decisively.

4

Once through the doorway, Bruna stood blinking and straining her eyes to see. The room was warm and dark like a cow byre. It smelt of grease, sweat and stale wine. All round the long tables, laden with pots and dirty platters, people joked and roared with laughter. There were torches placed high up on the walls and a steaming pot bubbled on the brazier.

When her eyes had become accustomed to the low light, Bruna threw the sides of her cloak over her shoulders and settled her companion on a bench by the door.

'Don't move until I return, my lady. I will seek out the innkeeper and ask after our room.'

The woman kept her head lowered and showed no reaction. Bruna shrugged her shoulders and turned away. The place certainly did not seem dangerous, and the customers were too busy eating and making merry to notice the two women who had arrived. Seeing a serving woman carrying pots of scalding hot wine, Bruna went over to her.

'My good woman, pray tell me where the innkeeper is. We have travelled far, and board and lodging has been arranged for us.'

'Well, I'd be surprised about that! We're full to the rafters, even in the stables! But, stay there, my dear, I'll be a-fetching of him all the same,' replied the old woman seeing Bruna's crestfallen expression.

Despite her age, the serving woman was still agile and, lifting up her petticoats, she climbed a ladder to the trap door that led to the upper floor. On the first floor was a communal dormitory

17

and two private bedrooms, one of which was the innkeeper's. The old woman ran over to it without a moment's hesitation and pressed her ear up to the door. She heard a series of deep moans. The master was certainly there . . . and not alone. She knocked loudly and heard a stream of abuse from inside the room. The old woman smiled, for once he was not cursing her. He must have wrestled the little new girl down onto the straw mattress. Anything would do for that fat oaf, so long as it wore petticoats and squealed underneath him.

'Who is it?' growled a hoarse voice.

'It is I, the old girl! There's some people as are here to see you, Master Guiraut!'

The innkeeper opened the door abruptly; his face was flushed scarlet and glistening with sweat, and his tunic was open.

'People! People! Strewth, what do I need with people? We're full. Can't you see I'm busy?'

'Two young ladies are a-waiting for you below,' replied the old woman, unabashed (and not displeased that she had interrupted the exploits of this master for whom she cared little).

'Two young ladies, you say?' he repeated, suddenly interested.

'Yes, master, proper ladylike ladies. They're a-saying that they've hired a room here.'

The man frowned and then tidied himself up, tying a wide belt round his huge paunch. He stood aside so that the skinny young girl could sidle past him, her torn tunic revealing wan skin and scantily covered bones.

'Go on, scram, Berthe. Get out and make it quick!' he said, applying a hefty thump to the girl's rump so that she sprawled to the floor of the landing.

'Let's go and see about this, old girl!'

He had hardly reached the foot of the ladder before discerning Bruna's hooded figure, and that of her companion, over by the door. He greeted her in what was meant to be a friendly way.

18

'A good day to you, and what can I do for you, my beauty?'

'I am not your beauty, innkeeper, I am the Untamed. We have come from Lord d'Apchon, who has arranged board and lodging for us in your house.'

The innkeeper, preoccupied as he was with trying to spy her face under the hood, scratched his chin and replied, 'But, you see we're full. Even if I wanted to, I could not take you in here.'

Bruna responded as if she had not even heard him and asked him frostily, 'You do not know Lord d'Apchon, do you, innkeeper?'

'Indeed yes. I do know him,' replied the other hesitantly.

'Everyone knows that he is not blessed with great patience. But do you know that not long ago, at Christmas-tide, I believe, one of his vassals made some mockery about his horse? The poor fellow had scarcely finished laughing before his master's ballock dagger was planted in his throat. And that was one of his friends . . . whereas you . . . !'

The man remained speechless. Bruna tackled him with another question, 'And now, what were you saying on the subject of our board and lodging?'

The innkeeper nodded silently, thinking on his feet to find a solution. He had hired out the private room booked for the women to two other pilgrims, thinking he could pocket the money twice.

'Did Lord d'Apchon ask you to give us board and lodging or did he not?'

'He did.'

'Well, then, take us to our room forthwith, my mistress is tired.'

'Uh, well, you will have to wait a few moments, because I thought that it would be most agreeable for you to stay in my own private room, it is the most comfortable. While we are installing a second mattress there, I will have some hot wine

19

brought over for you,' the innkeeper conceded grudgingly.

'Now, that's better,' said Bruna with a thin smile.

5

Despite the lateness of the hour, Le Puy's Notre-Dame cathedral was still full of faithful worshippers. The dying sunlight had deserted the lofty windows and had been succeeded by the feeble glow of oil lamps. An old priest hurried over to the sacristy and dropped to his knees a little way from the high altar. Here he was secluded from the crowd, protected from their stares by a tall pillar, as he bent his forehead to the ground and placed his palms on either side of his head, praying fervently.

Without a sound, a shadowy figure came and stood behind him and a soft voice spoke, making him jump in surprise, 'I must make my confession to you.'

'But—'

'I must, that is what is written and it is your duty to listen to me.'

The priest wanted to turn round to face the man, but the voice rang in his ears menacingly, 'Stand up, but do not turn round! I will speak in your ear. It is not always necessary to make one's confession in public, our Lord accepts confessions made like this, does he not?'

The priest rose, tilted his head and obeyed.

'You are right. I am listening, my son.'

'Never say that,' growled the voice.

'What did I say?'

'Don't say: my son!'

The old man swallowed hard and whispered, 'But then, what shall I call you?'

'No names, old man, no names.'

The voice fell silent. The priest did not dare turn round. He could feel the man's hot breath on his neck and he joined his hands together in a passive gesture of faith.

'You see,' the pilgrim spoke again, 'I need you to confirm what I have learned.'

'What is it that you have learned?'

'According to the Scriptures there is a great difference between a sin committed in the full knowledge that it is a sin, and one committed in ignorance.'

'That is true,' said the priest, wondering anxiously where the conversation was heading.

'I have also been told that a sin one could never have committed had one understood the enormity of it is venial, because it was committed in ignorance.'

'Yes, that is also true.'

'I was ignorant of my sin and I am dogged by remorse. I want to confess my sins and I am prepared to accept any penance you see fit to give me.'

'Very good, I am listening,' said the old priest, somewhat reassured by this sudden humility.

The man seemed to gather his strength before announcing in a distant voice, as if evoking something that had nothing to do with himself, 'For as long as I can remember, I have always hated – I have hated everyone, starting with my father. He was a man with great sturdy muscles, a man with hair more coarse than a wild boar's, a man who beat me like a dog. On the day of my sixteenth birthday he wanted to whip me and I sank my knife into his belly. I turned it round and round just as he had taught me. His guts spilled out onto his feet. That was the first and most difficult murder. Afterwards, I was frightened someone would find me and I fled—'

'Your sin committed in ignorance is your father's murder!' cried the priest.

'Silence, I have not finished! As I was saying, he was dead, but there was still my mother. A strumpet, a whore, who posed and pouted to everyone and anyone, even to me. I caught her in the arms of a rich merchant two weeks after my father was buried, and I killed them both there on the bed, pinned like bats to a door, with a long javelin through each of them! When I killed her lover my mother did not dare move. She probably thought I would spare her, the stupid hussy! Even in death, you could not tell whether it was the pain or the shock that made her look so hideous!'

'You killed your parents,' stuttered the old man, 'and you talk of venial sins?'

'Why, yes. At the time I was ignorant, I did not even go to Mass. I did not know about evil or about hell.'

The priest was feeling increasingly uncomfortable.

The other man went on bitterly, 'After that I could trust no one, I saw the Enemy even in the faces of young men, mere striplings, who gazed at me lovingly . . . but I did not force anyone. It was always they who came to me, putting their gentle hands on my shoulder, rubbing up against me—'

'But what are you talking about?' said the old priest, terrified by the mounting excitement in the man's voice.

'Of hell, old man, of hell!'

The priest involuntarily brought his hand to his chest where a pain that he knew only too well suddenly wracked him. He spluttered breathlessly, 'I can scarcely understand what you're saying, you're making my head spin. Who are these striplings you speak of?'

'Have you been listening to what I've been saying or are you deaf, priest?' growled the other. 'I want absolution!' The man's voice cracked with tension. He put his hands onto the old priest's shoulders, sinking his fingernails into the fabric of his robe. 'I need your forgiveness. It is not my fault if there is sin all around us! You know that He is the master of this world, do you not? You know it.'

The priest was silent. The man's fingers slipped towards his neck.

'Temptation is all around us, even here in this church!' cried the man as he tightened his grip.

'I can't breathe,' moaned the priest.

The pain was becoming unbearable. It had run down the length of his left arm, and was so strong it made him gasp for breath. In a desperate effort he tried to grab the hands that gripped him convulsively.

'I want absolution, priest!'

'I cannot give it,' croaked the priest.

The church spun round before the old man's eyes and he opened and closed his mouth like a fish out of water. He made a strange gurgling sound and slumped against the stranger.

'Any sin, even one that leads to damnation, can be pardoned by confession and contrition! It is written, do you hear me? I know it. It is written!'

The man suddenly seemed to become aware of the body in his arms, and he let it slip to the floor. A quick glance at the scarlet face was enough.

'Oh, for pity's sake, the old man's dead!'

Horrified, he looked round the dark nave, but could see no faces turned towards them.

'You're dead!' he murmured, hiding the unfortunate priest behind a pillar. 'You don't wish to help me, then! Well, I shall find someone who will, do you hear? I want absolution and I shall have it!'

The man walked off quite calmly and no one paid him any attention.

There were hundreds of pilgrims walking up and down the town's alleys, but the old priest's body lay alone in the shadowy chancel for a long time before a monk eventually noticed it.

6

It was now a week since Guillaume the mason and his family had laid down their meagre belongings in one of the cottages built of straw and clay in Saint-Jacques, an outpost of Le Puy that the locals had built outside the city walls specifically for sheltering pilgrims. Guillaume had come from the Blois region with his wife Bérengère and their son Garin. It had been a bad year for them, and Guillaume had heard from a fellow mason who had been to Compostela that it was easy to find work and set up home in Galicia. All the pilgrims, especially the craftsmen among them, who settled anywhere along the *camino francés* were promised their own plot of land and the freedom to exercise their skills – something they could not find anywhere else in the Frankish kingdom.

And so they had set off, knowing that the surest way of reaching Galicia was to travel with the pilgrims. Bérengère, a fervent Christian, had insisted that they go all the way to Compostela to ask for help from Saint Jacques, before settling somewhere along the *camino*.

'Garin, go and fetch me some water,' Bérengère asked her son.

'Yes, mother,' replied the young man, taking the pail from her.

Once outside, he huddled into his old mantle and rubbed his hands together vigorously. It was still cold, and plumes of condensation filled the air with his every breath. He was in the middle of an encampment of some twenty tents. Most of them stood empty because, with the tarpaulins flapping and rattling in the gusts of icy wind, the pilgrims had preferred to take refuge in the city itself or round the great fires that blazed in the main squares of this outpost.

'Mustn't complain,' thought Garin as he looked at the tents, 'we're lucky to be in a house. But once we're on the road, we'll all be buffeted by the same wind. We'll have to walk a long way and for a long time.'

Try as he might, Garin could not begin to imagine a journey of over 400 leagues! It was as good as going to the Holy Land; it was to the ends of the earth. They would travel beyond the mountain peaks capped in snow that never melted, where there were bears, eagles, wolves and even dragons if you believed everything you heard.

And all these people. Garin had never seen so many people all in one place, so many men in particular – there were only a few women and children. Among them were those who had already made the pilgrimage, immediately recognisable because of the *coquille Saint-Jacques*, the scallop shell stitched to their mantles or their hoods. That was what his old friend Humbert had told him. Humbert may have been old and poor but he had three scallop shells. Garin had met him at the fountain and still remembered the moment he had struck up a friendship with the old man.

It had snowed and, that morning, Garin had left early to go and fetch water. That was where he saw him. Humbert was trying in vain to break the ice with the metal tip of his walking stick.

'Can I help you?' Garin asked.

25

The man turned round, his eyes blazing.

'Do you think that you are stronger than I, boy?'

'Why no,' rejoined Garin brightly. 'But I think that together we would be stronger.'

A smile sketched itself onto the ageing pilgrim's face, giving him an unusually soft expression.

'What is your name?'

'Garin, at your service, my lord.'

'Well, you are right, Garin, and – at least on this occasion – you are wiser than old Humbert. Come, take this.' And the two men broke the ice together before clapping each other's hands in cordial salute, and going their separate ways. A gesture which, Garin was sure, had sealed their friendship.

Later Garin came to think of Humbert as both great and small. Great in presence and small in stature: the man was barely taller than himself and yet, when you looked at him, he stood so proud and square that he appeared tall.

His white hair was carefully combed and fastened with a cord. He wore a broad-brimmed hat, like the Flemish merchants. His beard was braided in the ancient manner, and there were three scallop shells stitched to his faded blue mantle. Three scallop shells meant three pilgrimages, three times 400 leagues. Garin was quite incapable of counting up to that.

One day had passed since their first meeting before Garin saw the old man again and addressed him politely, 'A good day to you, my lord Humbert, I would like to talk to you, if it so please you.'

Like the last time, Humbert eyed him sternly before softening when he recognised him.

'Oh, it is you. What do you want of me?'

'Your scallop shells, do they mean that you have made this pilgrimage three times?'

'No, my boy, it means that the pilgrimage has made me three

times.' And with these enigmatic words, which rolled round and round Garin's head all night, the old man had turned on his heels and walked off.

Garin had spent the whole of the next day looking for Humbert. At last he had found him living in a tent at the foot of the city's ramparts. He was sitting on his mattress carving the head of a walking stick.

'I understand now,' said Garin.

'What is it that you understand, my boy?'

'That this pilgrimage changes us.'

Humbert smiled and deigned to look up from his work.

'Yes, Garin, it changes us. Thanks to this pilgrimage, you will never be the same person again.'

'But you, why did you need to change three times?'

Humbert smiled.

'Because of the Infidels. By going to Compostela, the Christians drive them out of Iberia.'

'Are the Infidels really so close at hand?' exclaimed the young man. 'I thought they were in the Holy Land. Have they already crossed over the mountains?'

Humbert smiled indulgently.

'Oh no, Garin, they've been there a long time. The Muslims took most of Iberia nearly four hundred years ago.'

'Four hundred years!'

'My boy,' said the old man, indicating for him to sit down, 'do you know who Saint Jacques is? Do you know why you are setting off on this white path?'

'Uhh . . . not really.'

'Our Saviour called Saint Jacques "Bonaerges", and do you know what that means?'

'Indeed not.'

'It means son of thunder, because Jacques was loyal but impulsive, which pleased Jesus. He was one of the twelve apostles, one of the first to spread His word. He was an ardent follower and performed many miracles, and in return he was condemned to death by Herod Agrippa.'

'But how did Herod kill this son of thunder?'

'Bonaerges perished by the sword. His companions took his body, and their boat was steered by the winds to the coast of Galicia, not far from the port of Iria. The journey took only one night, a night like no other, a single night that was worth seven nights.'

'A night that was worth seven nights!' repeated Garin, who had dropped down at Humbert's feet and could not take his eyes off him, fascinated by his words.

'Yes,' Humbert continued, 'and Bonaerges's body was carried by wild bulls to the lands of the cruel queen Louve, where it was laid on a stone which melted around it like warm wax carving a strange sarcophagus for him. Years passed, then centuries, and eventually everyone forgot him. Then came the time of the Saracens and the time of Charlemagne. Much Frankish blood flowed, spilt by the Infidels.'

'And that's when the Infidels invaded Iberia!' declared Garin spiritedly.

'And that is when Bonaerges appeared. A hermit dreamed of him and guided by the twinkling of a star, he found the place where the tomb still stood, the *campus stellae* – the field of stars – Compostela. It is said that a man appeared on the battlefield then, a man in a halo of light riding a white horse. When he charged, leading valiant knights behind him, so fearless was he that he sowed terror among the Saracens and put them to flight. The son of thunder was back among men – and men, in their thousands, and for centuries since have taken the white path which leads to the field of stars.'

'That's the path we're going to follow, I understand, and four hundred leagues is not that far after all!' exclaimed Garin. 'Will we soon see the son of thunder, Humbert?'

'Perhaps, Garin. You have to have faith. But come and sit beside me and tell me about your people.'

And Garin sat down next to Humbert on his mattress, telling him of his father's poverty, the lack of work, their dream of settling in Galicia, the village he had left behind, his friends . . . he opened his heart more readily to this attentive old man than to any of his former comrades.

From time to time Humbert would nod, ask a question or encourage him to go on. Then Garin fell silent and the old man said to him abruptly, 'Take me to your father, my boy.'

That was how Humbert became involved with the mason's family, agreeing to guide them along the path he knew so well in exchange for a few meals taken with them.

'But who are you really, Humbert?' Garin asked him one day.

'A pilgrim, just a pilgrim.'

But the more Garin came to know him, the more surprised he became by the old man. Humbert could read and write, he understood several languages and spoke a number of different dialects.

A group of Flemish horsemen had raised their tent not far from the mason's cottage and, one morning, Garin had come across his ageing friend deep in conversation with them. When they parted, the horsemen had bid the old man farewell most earnestly. And this farewell was more a gesture of respect than a simple adieu.

'Humbert,' Garin said a little reproachfully, 'you have not trusted me with the truth. You are not a pilgrim, are you?'

'No, Garin, you are wrong. But perhaps the other day you asked me the wrong question.'

The young man thought and then said slowly, 'Who were you, Humbert?'

'A crusader, just a crusader, Garin.'

The young man's mouth dropped open in amazement and he let out a long whistle.

'You've been all the way to the Holy Land?'

'Yes, my boy.'

'Oh, Humbert, tell me, tell me everything.'

Humbert smiled.

'We have plenty of time, Garin. Have you forgotten that we are to travel four hundred leagues together?'

'No, Humbert but—'

'Patience, Garin,' said the old man. 'Patience.'

Then Garin met a woman. Not one like his mother who was worn down by work and by life itself, but a young damsel who wore breeches and carried a knife, and was a difficult character to boot. She had come to the encampment several times looking for something or someone, asking questions here and there. One day, unable to contain his curiosity, Garin spoke to her.

'What are you looking for, damsel? I could help you, I am sure of it.'

But the girl was not easily persuaded. Like Humbert, she had eyes which sparkled with spirit, only, in her, Garin found it appealing in a very different way.

'By my troth, you are quick to talk yourself up, boy.'

Garin gathered himself to his full height – he was a good head taller than her.

'I meant no offence, but I'm no childling! I have reached my seventeenth year, just as you have, I believe, and I am a man, damsel!'

The girl's tone softened, 'Very well. No offence taken. You see, I'm trying to find a *Jacquet*, and I cannot find a suitable one.'

'But there are so many of them here!'

'There are just a lot of people with shells on their clothes and plenty of rotten game,' muttered the girl.

'Oh, I can swear to you, damsel, that there is better than that.'

'Do you know someone then?'

'Why are you looking for a *Jacquet* in the first place?'

'Well, what a simpleton! To guide my mistress and myself to Compostela, why else?'

'Are you pilgrims, without husbands, or brothers, or family?'

'Yes, and stop opening your eyes so wide at me like that. Take me to this *Jacquet* that you know instead.'

'Oh, but he's not an easy type you know, and I don't think he'll be pleased if you talk to him like that!' said Garin rather stubbornly.

'First of all, how many scallop shells does he have, this *Jacquet* of yours?'

'Three, damsel. And I can tell you – but you are not to repeat it – that he's a crusader!'

'Take me to him,' said Bruna determinedly. 'I'm going to make him an offer that a great many people would accept.'

And Humbert accepted.

Garin never knew what she told him but Bruna and Humbert shook hands as they parted company. The old man watched the girl's slender figure for a long time as she walked away. The young man smiled. If Humbert had accepted her offer, that meant they would be travelling together . . . and that did not displease him in the least.

7

Since the old priest's death his murderer did not dare return to the cathedral, and he slunk around outside it with his hood lowered over his face, for fear of being recognised. He found it so difficult getting to sleep. Why would no one absolve him? What was written was written!

And there was the Enemy, too, crouching on every street corner. He hated towns, loathed them, with their crowds, their pillories and their gallows dangling dead bodies tormented by the crows.

He must get back to his work. He felt the weight of his blade in its sheath and he smiled, reassured. All this could be sorted out somewhere else, in the other world. And then he would be able to sleep for ever.

8

'It is cold, my lords, try some of my wine. It is better than the sun in winter, it'll warm up your hides and your very bones!' called a young man with a small barrel attached to his leather belt.

'Give me some,' said a little man with a thin face. 'Give me a goblet of that, my boy.'

'Yes, sire,' said the boy, swiftly filling the little pewter goblet that hung on a chain from his belt. 'That'll be one *sou*,' he added, handing it to the man.

The man took out a purse so flat that anyone would have believed it to be empty, and took from it a tiny coin which he offered to the boy.

'Here, take this, and I hope for your sake that your wine's as good as you say it is,' said the man downing the drink in one go.

'Would you like another one?' the trader asked him eagerly, drumming the icy ground with his foot.

'Pour away,' said the man, handing back the goblet.

As he filled the goblet a second time, the young boy scrutinised his customer. He was dressed in a mantle of brown cloth, splattered and stained by the snow, and he had a rebec slung across his shoulder. A *trouveur*, then, and not a young man, and not a wealthy man.

'Are you a *Jacquet*, sire?' asked the boy inquisitively.

'If you like.' The man sighed. 'At the moment I'm merely a wanderer, and one wearied by too long a road, at that.'

'Have you come to sing before the bishop?'

'What is it to you what I am here for, boy?' asked the man heatedly.

'My apologies, I did not intend to offend you. But you spoke of a long journey, where have you come from?'

'From hell!' replied the other. 'Find me somewhere to stay for the night rather than baiting me with your questions.'

Realising that the man was at the end of his tether, the young boy muttered an apology and then exclaimed, 'But everywhere's full here! If you'll believe me, sire, there is no room left even in the cathedral. You will have to go to the Saint-Jacques township, outside the city walls, that's where all the pilgrims are.'

'Which is the best hostel?' the man asked suddenly, without paying any attention to the young trader's words.

'But I've just said—'

'Which is the best hostel? Answer me!'

'The one in the rue Rochetaillade,' said the boy quietly.

'Take me there.'

'But what about my trade?' protested the boy.

'Take me there!' growled the man, grabbing his arm and crushing it in his tense grasp. 'Didn't your father teach you to be quiet and do as you were told?'

'Hey, let me be, sire, I'll be a-taking you there.'

'Now, that's better,' said the man gloomily.

9

'How can I say this more clearly? I don't have a cot, or so much as a mattress to spare!' cried the innkeeper Guiraut.

'You don't have a mattress for Ronan, the rebec player?' the man replied haughtily. 'I, the *trouveur*, shall sing for you and fill your tavern with more customers than any other in town! You'll be turning people away or sitting them down in the snow! From misty England to the distant Orient, there is no one better than I!'

Guiraut thought for a moment and then a crafty expression crept across his face. He had an idea: the *trouveur* could have two uses, he would bring in more custom and, on top of that, he would help him get his revenge on that arrogant female, Bruna. He had seen her go out a little earlier; she would have a bit of a surprise on her return.

'Yes, I do have something for you, but you will not be on your own.'

'Splendid. Do you really believe that in my travels to the very ends of the earth, I have often had a room to myself?'

'Well, let's shake on it, and now follow me,' said Guiraut climbing to the upper floor.

The innkeeper went over to a door and, without knocking, opened it and stood aside to let Ronan into the room. There were already two cots in the narrow room under the eaves, and one of them was occupied by a silent figure under a blanket. The man jumped in surprise.

'My word, it is a woman!' he said, seeing the sleeper's profile.

'Indeed yes. She is a little simple. She will not object to your sleeping here.'

'And whose is the other cot? Her husband's?'

'No, some mountain girl, a wild creature.'

Ronan nodded his head and went over to the motionless form.

'You take great liberties with your clients. We should at least wake this lady and ask her mind.' He bent over the motionless body and exclaimed, 'But she's not even sleeping! Her eyes are open. She looks dead.'

'Fie, she is deaf or dumb.'

'My lady, my lady!' said the troubadour, touching the woman's shoulder.

But she neither replied nor reacted. Ronan turned to the innkeeper with a questioning expression.

'That's what I told you. I'll have a mattress brought up for you,' the innkeeper said as he left.

Once his mattress had arrived, the troubadour shut the door and, with a shrug of his shoulders, let himself drop down onto his bed. He was too exhausted to think and, even though he was disconcerted by the innkeeper's behaviour, at least it meant that he had board and lodging until the time came to leave.

In that dark space under the eaves it was mortally cold, but what he needed most was to sleep. He laid his rebec down beside him, slipped his knife under his arm and, with one last glance at the motionless woman on the next cot, wrapped himself in his mantle and went straight to sleep.

He was woken by a soft sound, but it was already too late, there was a blade at his throat.

'Who are you? What are you doing in our room?' hissed a furious voice.

The man half opened his eyes. The voice belonged to the prettiest girl he had seen for a long time. Oh, not one of your town beauties, oh no. A girl with beautiful almond eyes, high cheekbones and long black shiny hair. He remembered that the innkeeper had mentioned a wild girl from the mountains and he replied coolly, 'Hi, hi, gentle damsel, I shall reply if you stop prodding me with your cursed knife.'

The girl hesitated and then eased the pressure off the man's throat.

'Who are you?' she said again.

'My name is Ronan de Bretagne, damsel, and I am a *trouveur*.'

'De Bretagne? You must be from Brittany, whereabouts in Brittany?'

'From the ends of the earth.'

The girl seemed to consider this and lowered her blade a little further.

'Why are you here?'

'The innkeeper put me here, saying that you would not mind. I have travelled far, if it so please you, damsel, that is the reason for my presence in this palace of icy draughts, my princess!'

Her eyes blazing with rage, Bruna whistled between her teeth.

'That pig, I'll make him pay for this! I'm most aggrieved for your sake, but you cannot stay here. I am responsible for my lady's protection and well-being, so—'

'In other circumstances, damsel, I would willingly obey you, but today I have such need of bed and board, and the innkeeper offered it to me, so I'm staying!'

'No, you are leaving! How much do you want? I can pay.'

Ronan's face broke into a mocking smile.

'I would not leave you for all the treasures in Byzantium or far off Tartarie, fair damsel. Your eyes have captured me and chained me to this miserable mattress – fear nothing, then, from your humble slave, I beg you!'

The young girl bit her lips and thought. If she drove this one out, the burly Guiraut would only send her up another, and probably someone worse.

'I can see full well that you are mocking me and that you are more mad than dangerous. On no account are you to come any closer to us, and all will be well,' she said, putting away her knife.

The troubadour gave no reply and, turning to face the wall, pulled his hood over his face. Bruna hesitated a few moments until loud snores reverberated from the *trouveur*. She smiled in spite of herself, and sat down on her cot. There was just one night left before the great departure, after all.

10

When Ronan woke, the Sexte Mass was being rung in at the cathedral and he found himself alone in the room. He stretched and, looking about him, saw a bathing basin and a jug of water on the matting that covered the floor. He took off his clothes and took a package of linen from his travelling bag which was wrapped around a strop, a razor, a mirror of polished pewter and a box made of boxwood which contained a slither of saponin soap.

After pouring a little water in the basin, he stood in it and soaped his hair and body at length before rinsing himself off. Then, standing over by the window, he shaved carefully, guided by his reflection in the pewter mirror. Finally, he took clean breeches and a clean tunic from his bag, put them on and sighed with satisfaction.

'I feel better. A bit of snow is no match for some warm water and a good soaping! Now I must go and pay my respects to Our Lady, and this evening I will earn my keep in the room below.'

A little later, after downing a meagre meal and settling up with the innkeeper, Ronan joined the throng of pilgrims and found himself propelled to the top of the rue des Tables at the foot of the cathedral. Its tall frontage loomed over him with its mosaic of white stone and red lava. Despite the snow that clung to the cornices, the gloomy building still retained its aura of mystery, as if it belonged more to Byzantium than to the Frankish kingdom.

All around him were scores of men and women who seemed to have come from every corner of Christendom. He could hear them speaking in many different dialects: Breton, Poitevin, Provençal, Flemish . . . Monks from the bishop's palace passed up and down the rows of worshippers, handing out bread, onions and wine. Peasants heaved straw bales from carts to make up mattresses for the pilgrims to sleep on inside the cathedral.

Ronan spoke to one of the young peasants, asking him how he could get to the high altar. He replied with a smile, 'Oh it be not difficult, sire, you go into the church of Notre-Dame through the navel and you come out through the ears! Let the crowd carry you, you'll see for yourself!'

Ronan thanked him and, following his advice, slipped into the crowd of the faithful and was swept in through a pair of doors covered in dazzling panels of polished copper. He was surprised to see that they were engraved with interlaced Arabic letters in among the Latin inscriptions.

A long stairway, cluttered with traders offering religious amulets and medallions, led him directly to the black Virgin. The nave was so crowded that he had to step over the faithful who lay on the very paving slabs. The entire building echoed with chanting and whispered prayers. A little further on, a group of wealthy townspeople stood talking business with some canons. Overhead, vast oriental domes replaced the usual arches of stone. Ronan felt that this was all strangely familiar, as though he were in some country in the Orient, the Orient he had so loved.

That was when he saw Bruna: she was kneeling before the black Virgin, praying fervently, her long black hair brushing the paving stones. When she stood up, he made up his mind, he would follow her. This strange girl attracted him in spite of himself but, even though he tried to ignore it, this attraction was tempered with curiosity.

She left the cathedral by the porchway dedicated to Saint Jacques and, having passed in front of the baptistry, went down the rue de Séguret towards the little fortified village of Aighuilhe. She walked quickly and went straight to the outer door of the Séguret Abbey.

There were monks standing watch at the door, calming the impatient pilgrims with the help of sturdy wooden sticks. Ronan slipped through a doorway and found himself in the abbey's courtyard. A new chapel was being built and there was a hospital as well as some buildings reserved for the monks, but the *trouveur* paid these scant attention. He had eyes only for the rocky peak that rose before him. He stepped forward slowly, fascinated by this dark jutting rock face, and the tiny church and clock tower perched on top of it.

It was such a peculiar, haunting place that he quite forgot to watch the young woman. He noticed that steps had been carved into the rock and that, despite the icy blasts of wind, there were pilgrims gripping the rock face and climbing to the peak. As if in a dream, he found himself at the foot of the crag of Aighuilhe, and he too began to climb.

The rock glistened with molten snow, and from time to time he slipped and, to save himself from falling, had to grasp the ropes that the Séguret monks had fastened along the way. Ronan looked up and saw Bruna climbing the steep incline with great assurance like a young goat.

The higher the young man climbed, the more potently he felt that he was leaving the earth behind, as if this strange place had the power to guide him towards the heavens. A few lines from Jacob's dream surfaced in his memory:

> . . . and behold a ladder set up on the earth, and the top of it reached to heaven: and behold the angels of God ascending and descending on it.

Above him an ageing pilgrim slipped, startling him awake from his meditations. Ronan only just managed to catch the pilgrim and save him from what would have been a fatal fall. He led him to one of the few ledges which allowed the faithful climbers to catch their breath. There were nooks carved into the rocks behind these ledges; he later learned that these places, here on this outcrop of rock battered by the hostile wind, housed the bones of the past abbots.

Ronan stopped on the last landing before reaching the little church and looked round. The view was extraordinary. A long line of leaden clouds emphasised the horizon like a stroke of black ink. In the distance he could make out the hazy blue outline of the high mountain peaks and, looking down, he could see the entire city at his feet.

The *trouveur* turned round and looked more closely at the rock face which was embellished with mosaics, and the lintel which featured two mermaids facing one another. A few more steps took him into the sanctuary. He moistened his fingers in a font fed by the waters from the sky, and stepped on towards the oratory and its high altar, covered in a simple cloth of white linen.

The walls were covered in magnificent paintings in glowing colours, depicting Saint Michael, the knight of Our Lord, to whom the chapel was dedicated. On the section of wall behind the altar the painting was of a spiral of bluish cloud, where angels trod softly, leading the dead towards the light and the resurrection. Ronan was swept up into a dream, leading him to the distant Orient, and his thin mouth twisted into a bitter sneer.

He shook himself out of his reverie. Tomorrow was the great day of departure, and he had to think of ways of gathering a few *deniers* together for the journey.

11

After these days of intense cold, the sun rose over the town of Le Puy, illuminating the procession winding its way round the town. The great Pascal Mass was about to begin. Children ran pell-mell in the streets, screeching with excitement, announcing the arrival of the cortège. Horsemen armed with tall lances opened up a pathway, forcing onlookers to scatter and make way for the Virgin.

Carried by six sturdy monks on a litter covered in gleaming scarlet silk, the black Virgin of Le Puy, Sancta Maria de Podio, was the centre of attention. Her body was entirely wrapped in strips of cloth, making her look like some Egyptian deity on the road to everlasting life. Her fine black face was circled by a headband covered in precious stones, and she held her son, the child Jesus, before her.

People signed themselves with the cross or threw themselves to the ground as the litter passed by. Here, just as in Chartres, they were more ready to worship the Virgin than God himself.

After climbing up the rue des Tables, the procession finally arrived back before the heavy doors of Notre-Dame cathedral. Pilgrims and monks alike vigorously intoned the *salve regina*. Behind the Virgin came the bishop and the canons along with the other high dignitaries. Their cloaks, lined with ermine and grey squirrel, bore witness to the riches enjoyed by men of the church. Behind them came the barons and the viscounts, followed by a host of knights and their squires. There was a strange contrast between these gold-edged chasubles and fur-lined capuchons, and the sober dark cloaks of the pilgrims who brought up the rear of the procession.

Monks armed with heavy sticks parted those faithful followers who were a little too impetuous, and the huge cortège processed into the cathedral. The bishop Pierre III had arranged everything with great care. As well as the clear sunlight pouring down from the domes, little oil lamps had been put in every dark corner along the nave and in the apses, diffusing a rare golden glow over the magnificent stonework.

The lords and ladies took up their position before the high altar. The men of God took their places in the choir. As for the pilgrims, there were so many of them that the cathedral could scarcely contain them all, and some were left kneeling outside the porch.

There was a fervour and a tension in the air peculiar to the last days before this great departure to Compostela. A departure which, for many, would be without return, because the white path was the death of many a pilgrim. But each and every one of them was ready. They wore knee-length doublets over their breeches, and hooded mantles to protect them from the cold and the rain. Their only belongings were contained in small pouches and purses. On the end of each long staff was carried a calabash of water. Many set off barefoot to travel the hundreds of leagues that separated them from Galicia.

At the end of the Mass, the bishop plied a pathway through the crowds to the doors. Behind him came the monks, distributing mantles and staffs to those pilgrims who had none. Pierre III walked through the kneeling *Jacquets*, repeating the traditional blessing:

'In the name of Our Lady, take this staff and this mantle, the symbols of thy pilgrimage, that thee may be worthy of reaching Saint Jacques's tomb purified, safe and enriched, and that, thy journey done, thee may return to us in perfect health.'

12

The inhabitants of Le Puy thronged at the gates of the town and on the ramparts to watch the *Jacquets* leave. Fathers took their children on their shoulders, youngsters scrambled onto the roofs, and they all watched the interminable procession of pilgrims, this people of God setting off for distant Iberia.

The column of faithful already stretched away to the Margeride mountains in the distance. The wind had lifted again, whipping up flurries of snow. Soon they were just a black shadow on the horizon. Then nothing.

The following morning the lifeless body of a young nobleman was found in a filthy little back street, and the horribly mutilated corpse of an adolescent by the ramparts. It bore so many wounds that it seemed as though a blade might have danced upon it, emptying the poor man of his blood.

PART TWO

Deo Jublia.
Clero canta.
Daemones fuga.
Errantes revoca.

(Be jubilant to the Lord. Sing unto the clerics.
Chase out the demons. Bring back to the fold those
that have strayed.)

Inscription on the bell
in the dome at Aubrac

13

The sound of the horn, indicating Baron de Peyre's return, had echoed from one sentry post to another all the way along the Gévaudan. The guards stood on the tops of the ramparts watching the band of horsemen emerging from the horizon.

An icy wind blew across the plain, making the standards whip and crack. Despite the thin layer of snow that covered the frozen ground, the hammering of galloping hooves grew ever louder, and then the hoarse sound of the baron's trumpet suddenly blared above their thundering rhythm. The chargers leapt up the rise that led to the castle wall, and the watchmen raised the first portcullis. Now they could see the horsemen's hauberks and their glinting weapons. The mask-like hoods protecting the horses' heads gleamed with metallic menace.

There were some thirty mounted men led by the ageing baron, who could be identified instantly by the impressive standard he bore in his iron-clad hand as a sign of his rank. They clattered under the first portcullis and, without slowing their pace, encouraged their mounts to continue climbing towards the drawbridge in the inner wall.

They erupted into the castle's courtyard and dismounted in front of the bailiff and his serving men. A monk, who acted as the castle's chaplain and confessor, stood a few paces back waiting to greet the baron once he had dismounted. The master took off his helmet and handed it, and the standard, to one of his squires. He shook his mane of grey hair and ran one hand through his beard, a characteristic gesture of his. His face and eyes were red with cold.

After a swift glance round, he nodded his greetings to the man bowing to him, before turning to his escort. Stable boys had come to lead away the chargers which steamed and ran with sweat under their leather caparisons. The horsemen laid their lances and other arms against a wall.

The bailiff came over and bowed as he said, 'Welcome, Baron. I must speak to you without delay—'

But his master waved him away impatiently.

'Later, later! We will speak after we have bathed and sat at table.'

His tone implied that he was not to be crossed and, despite his anxiety, the bailiff did not dare press the point. He knew that this master was not one to be challenged or contradicted, because it made him as wild and as furious as an injured boar.

The baron turned to one horseman whose crimson shield indicated that he was not from his own household, and hailed him, 'Come, my lord Galeran. Come! A good fire awaits us within, and all we need to make us look like true men again.'

'Your castle has a proud bearing, Baron. Upon my word, it is a true eagle's nest!' exclaimed the chevalier, looking up towards the massive keep looming above them.

'Wait until you climb up there, Galeran. The roof is so high up that you can navigate upon the clouds!'

A flight of steps took the baron and his men to the lower hall inside the keep. The room had only two narrow arrow slits of natural light, but it was well lit by quantities of torches set high upon the walls. This was a man's retreat, and Galeran thought to himself that he had not yet seen a single woman or child. A row of multicoloured standards hung from the vaulted ceiling, and various weapons were displayed along the walls.

A long table stood before a huge deep chimney where half a

tree trunk blazed. The high flames lit up the flagstones on which two white greyhounds lay asleep. The dogs looked up, watching their master with their large black eyes, without moving or showing any sign of pleasure.

'They are always so,' said the baron, stroking the animals' superb necks. 'They do not like me to leave without them, and they like to show their discontent on my return. Come, my lord Galeran,' he added, 'I promised you some time to restore yourself before the pleasures of the table.'

A stone bench stood in one corner of the hearth, and there was a little oak door on the other side. The baron pushed it open and stood aside to let the young chevalier pass.

14

The two men came into a small chamber in which the warm steamy air smelt of lavender and rosemary. There were openings along the foot of the walls wafting hot air into the room.

'My steam room!' said the baron, smiling at the chevalier's astonishment. 'The chimney heats this little room even more efficiently than it does the great hall.'

An elderly serving woman in a blue kirtle stood, with her arms folded, over by two great wooden tubs filled with steaming water.

'You may treat this as your own home, Galeran, and my faithful Laune will look after you as she would my own self,' said the baron with an expansive wave of his hand.

'Great thanks to you, Baron, for your hospitality,' replied the chevalier with a bow. 'This will be most welcome after such a cold week of riding.'

The old baron, helped by the servant, took off his doublet and breeches, revealing a short, well-muscled torso like that of a young man. Scores of scars bore testimony to his ardours in battle and on the hunting field. He immersed himself in one of the tubs with a sigh of contentment and then instructed the old woman to look after his guest.

Having removed his clothes, Galeran climbed into the tub provided for him and sat down on the soft felt that lined the bottom. Laune lathered his back and rubbed it vigorously with a horse-hair brush. The chevalier began to relax: he could feel the tension in his muscles melting away in the good woman's expert hands.

All too soon the two men, duly soaped and scrubbed, regretfully climbed out of the tubs. The aged Laune massaged them again with oil blended with cinnamon and thyme. The weariness, which had weighed them down after their long days of riding through the cold and snow, left them.

The servant brought fresh linen in a willow basket and departed silently after handing her master and his guest clean shifts, breeches and two long ceremonial doublets.

'To the table!' cried the baron gleefully. 'I cannot bear my hunger a moment longer!'

'It is true, my lord,' replied the chevalier with a smile. 'I feel quite ready to do your generosity justice, as if I had not eaten for a week! Your steam room and your good Laune's ministrations have certainly restored me.'

When they entered the communal hall, many faces turned towards them. Among these Galeran recognised the knights from their escort, but there were a number of other vassals whom he did not know.

Silence descended around the high table, and the baron invited Galeran to sit down on his right, then the entire

50

assembly also sat down, having noisily greeted their master, crying, 'Long live the baron! Long live the baron!'

The sumptuous white cloths were laid with platters of precious metal, and silver knives and spoons. As was the custom, each person shared his platter with his neighbour. A silver-gilt spice box and a finely worked salt cellar were given pride of place in front of the master of the house.

The carvers placed a goodly slice of bread before the chevalier; then a cup-bearer came by carrying two ewers, one filled with water, the other with wine. He went over to the baron who indicated that he should serve his guest first.

'Not too much water,' said Galeran who had little liking for diluted wine.

'You are quite right, Chevalier,' announced the baron with a laugh, 'this wine is a Saint-Pourçain and I too like to drink it pure. I know no better wine, even the wine in Paradise could not compare to it!'

Galeran smelled the wine in his goblet, noting appreciatively its nose and vivid colour. Then he raised his goblet to honour his host and declared spiritedly, 'May God protect the baron and this whole noble assembly!'

The baron's men drummed the table with their fists to show their approval and, amidst the roar of conversation and jokes, the banquet began. At a signal from the bailiff, a long line of squires came in carrying many dishes tinted yellow with saffron and red with sandalwood. On the bailiff's orders, the cook had paid special attention to the colour of the food and, in honour of the baron, had only used yellow, which represented intelligence, and red dragon's blood to symbolise the baron's victorious strength.

The very first serving dish was filled with a steaming broth, and at the same time the diners were given Norse pâté and peppered chicken breast with their bread. Bowls of sauces were

51

offered, flavoured with a verjuice of grain and vinegar. Next came a rich stew of coney and a medley of salted fish. Despite their costliness, spices were available in great quanities around this table fit for a duke, and underlings ran hither and thither fetching extra salt and bread from the kitchen.

When eventually the sweet wine arrived along with a selection of delicate sweetmeats and pastries, the baron, who was not a great admirer of this tail end of a meal, pushed back his chair and turned to his neighbour.

'What was that priest from Vézelay saying to you, Galeran?' he asked gravely. 'Can we expect to see a new expedition to the Holy Lands?'

'I was just thinking about that,' replied the chevalier. 'We all know that since the fall of Edessa some two years ago, Louis VII has decided to take the Cross, but I had not expected Bernard de Clairvaux's words to inflame the knights so. It would seem that a second Crusade will soon be a reality, my dear Baron.'

The old lord glanced sideways at his guest. The blue-eyed chevalier from Brittany looked thoughtful, and the long scar that ran along his forehead furrowed deeply as he concentrated on his inner thoughts.

The two men had met at Vézelay ten days previously. They had attended the Easter sermon which, that year, had drawn the king himself and most of the vassals of his kingdom. The baron had taken an instant liking to the austere-looking young chevalier who had introduced him to Bernard de Clairvaux, and had suggested that he should follow him back to his estate after the great Mass.

Galeran, who liked the baron's uncompromising nature, accepted his invitation. The Mass was scarcely over before the baron's escort set off on its journey. Neither of the men wanted to stay in Vézelay. They each felt a need to distance themselves from the disruption that Bernard de Clairvaux's words had provoked.

In the space of a week, allowing their mounts little rest, they had reached Nevers and then Clermont, before setting off across the mountains of the Auvergne towards Aubrac and the Gévaudan.

'I must say, this Bernard de Clairvaux is a tough man,' observed the baron, running his hand through his beard. 'It is better, I don't doubt, to have him as a friend than an enemy.'

Galeran smiled a little sadly.

'Indeed, as with Abelard, no one recovers from an attack from him.'

'I have heard that said. But he is a great orator all the same.'

'And soldier,' added Galeran. 'I sometimes believe that the sword would have suited him better than the cloth. And yet, he has the word and that is just as mighty a weapon. Did you see how he tore his robes to make crosses of cloth! And the way he accorded his forgiveness with such fervour? "Take this cross of cloth," he said. "The cloth may cost little, but it has a great price: it will give you the Kingdom of God!"'

'Very few chevaliers were able to resist . . . except you, Galeran.'

'And you, Baron!' replied the chevalier with a sly smile.

The old nobleman's face lit up. He most certainly did like this particular companion. What a pity that he was not one of his trusty followers. He pushed back his chair, as he stood up, and gave the young chevalier a jovial thump.

'Come, my lord, I have something to show you.' He opened a doorway that revealed a little spiral staircase, picked up a torch and passed in front of the chevalier. As they climbed up, the old baron indicated the doors which opened onto each of the three floors, and explained that these were his and his men's quarters.

When they arrived at the top, the baron led Galeran over to

the crenellated ramparts. A blast of icy wind pinned them momentarily to the parapet, and the chevalier had the strange sensation that he was leaving the realms of men to join the eagles and sparrowhawks.

Watchmen, who had not even looked away from their duties when they heard the visitors arrive, kept vigil over the vast expanse that lay at their feet. The castle was built on a naked outcrop of rock, the roc de Peyre. It dominated the surrounding plateau, and no one could approach it from any direction without being spotted.

'Well, well, baron, you did not speak false,' said Galeran admiringly. 'You are quite unassailable here.'

Beaming with pride, the old baron held out his arm.

'Look, that is Aubrac, and there are the Causses mountains and the Margeride. On a clear day, we can even see the hills of the Auvergne and the jagged peaks of Aigoual. From here my watchmen can see the smooth running of my lands and much more besides . . .'

A discreet coughing sound made both men look round.

'Sire, I really must speak with you,' said the bailiff who had followed them. 'You really must hear me now, I beg you.'

The baron frowned.

'This is not like you to insist thus, Guyot,' he scolded. 'You usually wait for me to call you.'

The old bailiff lowered his head.

'It is something of the utmost importance,' he said, 'and time is short. If you had not come back so swiftly, I would have sent word to you in Vézelay.'

The baron sensed that this was indeed a serious matter to which he must attend. Galeran was about to withdraw discreetly, but he held him back.

'Stay, Chevalier, I have no secrets. Speak, Guyot, we are listening.'

54

'We have found two youngsters dead, my lord.'

'Well, yes, this can happen, alas! Dead of the cold, I don't doubt?'

'Indeed not, my lord, dead by the knife, and most hideously, you may have my word on it,' said the bailiff.

'On my lands?' snarled the baron. 'Speak, Guyot, who were these young men?'

'The first was found near the toll bridge at Estrets, my lord, but no one in the hamlet knows him. The second under the bridge at Marchastel, he was one of our shepherds.'

The old man swallowed hard as the bailiff continued, 'Of course, when I heard about the one at Estrets – that was two days ago – I set off straight away with a handful of men. You see, there were a great many people going through the toll gate because of the pilgrimage. One of the sergeants found him.'

'The pilgrimage?' Galeran asked.

'Yes, Chevalier,' intervened the baron. 'The *Jacquets* from Le Puy pass through my land and over the bridge at Estrets. It is not a heavy toll, and the pilgrims prefer crossing there than in the icy waters of the Truyère.'

'The path of stars, stars blotted with blood, just as the Moor woman predicted!' Galeran murmured, devastated.

As if through a mist, he heard the baron's voice continuing gruffly, 'Between the bridge and Aumont we're on the old Roman road, the *via Agrippa*. I, therefore, have armed men there all the time, because there is the most enormous number of pilgrims. There's a bit of everything in that crowd, and they do not always pass through without accident or incident among our locals . . . Right, keep talking, Guyot, we are listening.'

'The sergeant found this boy in the rocks near la Truyère. He was about fifteen. He'd been mutilated, my lords, as if by evil thieves. His tongue and his parts had been cut off, and his entire

55

body was slashed. His blood was clotted and frozen on the rocks around him . . .'

'You said that this boy was not local,' interrupted Galeran.

'Indeed, because there is only one family by the bridge, and they have no children.'

'Are there no other villages around the toll?'

'Yes, just one, but it is not very close by.'

'What is its name?' asked Galeran.

'Saint-Alban.'

'It would be wise to send someone there to make sure that we are not dealing with a local boy or a seasonal worker.'

'It shall be done, my lord,' said the bailiff, nodding.

This confounded chevalier was impressive; he could not say why, but the bailiff sensed that he was an unusually determined man. And that white scar on his forehead . . . this man had seen death at close hand and had surely not come back from such a meeting without some learning and wisdom.

'What did you do with the body?' asked Galeran.

'We covered it with stones, my lord, I did not want to leave it in that state, at the mercy of wild beasts.'

'And the other one?'

'The shepherd from Marchastel? A good man, I know his family. That is why I wanted to send word to you,' stammered the bailiff with feeling. 'He was like the other one.'

'What do you mean?' growled the baron.

'I mean that he had been tortured just as if they were brothers in blood and in death!'

'Where is he now? Have you buried him?' asked Galeran.

'No, my lord Chevalier, he is here in the castle chapel.'

15

Apart from a stone altar and two benches, the little chapel was quite empty of furniture. A statue of the Virgin, carved in wood as black as the night, stood in a recess next to an oil lamp that burned night and day.

The young shepherd's body had been covered in a ragged piece of cloth and laid on a trestle facing the altar. The chaplain was kneeling before it in prayer. The sound of the door opening made him look up, but the baron indicated that he should stay as he was, and went over to lift up the sheet. He stepped back slightly at the sight of the body, and he turned to Galeran saying in a muted voice, 'Look, chevalier! who could do such a thing?'

Galeran bent over the body in turn.

'Did you clean him, Father?' he asked the chaplain who had come over to join them.

'No, I think it was his family, my lord. He was like this when he was brought to me.'

'Thank you, Father.' He turned to the baron to ask, 'Would you allow me to examine him?'

'Yes, Chevalier,' said the old lord. 'Not only will I allow you to do so, but I swear before God and the Virgin who lives within these walls that I will pursue and chastise whomsoever did this!'

'Could you leave me alone in the chapel, Baron, and forbid anyone from entering?'

The baron frowned.

'I will wait for you outside, and no one will disturb you, Chevalier.'

Once the door was closed, Galeran turned towards the corpse

and drew the cloth back completely. The young man's body was absolutely naked and covered in so many wounds that they could not be counted. His skin was ashen, almost grey, so much of its blood had been shed.

Galeran ran the palm of his hand over the body, looking closely at the lips and the depth of each wound.

'Not one of these wounds is mortal,' he muttered angrily, 'whoever did this wanted above all to cause suffering.'

Then the chevalier lifted the eyelids, as if the man's staring, horrified eyes might reveal the image of his torturer. Looking between the shepherd's lips, he saw the stump of his tongue: he had been condemned to silence as well as to pain. His parts had been sliced off from his groin, probably after he was dead.

Galeran stood up and slowly drew a sign of the cross. So angry was he that his head was spinning and the blood was hammering behind his temples. He seized the ragged sheet and covered the body with it again, forcing himself to breathe evenly.

He had already seen many a body, and even the bodies of children not that long ago, the year before in fact, in Brittany.* But there was something more at play here: a desire to cause suffering and something darker still. His anger would not abate. He went out and, closing the chapel door more violently than he had intended, drank in the chill air outside.

The baron, who had been pacing up and down while he waited for him, came over to him and looked at him inquiringly. The chevalier shook his head, but said not a word.

* See *A Black Romance*.

58

16

'What do you think, Galeran?' asked the baron as soon as they were back in the great hall.

The chevalier went over to the chimney and, at his host's invitation, sat down on the stone bench. The fire was dying in the hearth, reduced to large red and black embers. The ageing baron paced backwards and forwards across the room as if made restless by his anger.

'I have heard tell of your talents, Chevalier. Bernard de Clairvaux even waxed rather too lyrical about them. You must help me find the culprit! You must, do you hear me? There is in these two deaths a feeling of evil that I will not tolerate.'

'I will help you, Baron.'

The chevalier's voice was resolute. His answer was as good as a promise and the baron knew this instinctively.

'Tell me what you think.'

'I believe, Baron, that – contrary to what your bailiff was saying – these murders were not committed by roadside thieves. The first fellow may have been from these parts or, and this is what I think, a pilgrim. In any event, a poor man. As for the second, he was a young shepherd, a poor man too.'

The chevalier paused.

'And even if we concede that whoever killed them might only have wanted food or a few meagre coins, there are the wounds . . .'

'What about the wounds?'

'A thief might kill in order to take a purse or even a knob of bread. But these wounds were made for the blood itself!'

'What do you mean?' asked the baron.

'Not one of them would have killed a man, except the last. But I think that the shepherd was dead before that, dead from the pain and emptied of his blood,' replied Galeran hoarsely.

'Who or what, then, are we dealing with?'

'An evil-doing beast, Baron, a creature of Satan which represents a mortal danger and one which I believe is following the white path to Compostela.'

The baron banged his fist against the lintel of the chimney.

'This monster made a mistake when it chose to kill on my lands, and to kill those to whom I should give my protection – be they pilgrims or shepherds, it matters not. He will pay for this, by my faith!' And, as if calmed by his own words, the baron turned towards the chevalier and said, 'Galeran, may I count on your succour?'

'By God, indeed you may,' replied Galeran solemnly. 'I give you my word.'

17

It was now seven days since the *Jacquets* had left Le Puy. After a few hours' walking, the City of the Virgin had disappeared behind them as the sun is swallowed up by the sea in the evening, and only the memory of its taverns remained to warm the pilgrims' thoughts.

The long column had stretched and broken up. Groups had formed, each walker falling in with companions whose pace suited their own. The few who travelled on horseback had drawn to the front before disappearing altogether, carried forwards by their steeds' powerful hocks.

It had started to snow again, a thick fall of snow which formed walls of white cloth between the pilgrims, silencing their songs and their laughter. In seven exhausting days the pilgrims had successively crossed the mountains of Devès, the gorges at Allier, the dark forests of Gévaudan and the plateaus of Margeride before joining the ancient *via Agrippa* at the bridge at Estrets.

The wind had been so icy cold that their clothes had stiffened on their bodies, and their sweat and breath had settled as a layer of frost on their faces. Those among the *Jacquets* who travelled barefoot and without gloves, had watched their extremities turning blue, and could now no longer feel them.

As they came into the Baron de Peyre's lands, the blizzard had abated a little. To bolster their spirits, the pilgrims had started intoning vigorous marching songs, accompanied here and there along the way by the incisive notes of a reed pipe.

18

On that particular evening the little group led by Humbert had found shelter for the night in a Benedictine priory in the fortified town of Aumont.

'We must sleep well and eat our fill,' the old *Jacquet* had said, 'because tomorrow will be a difficult day. The Aubrac forests contain as many brigands and wolves as they do tree trunks.'

They had all obeyed willingly, only too pleased to have found a safe place to spend the night.

When Bruna woke the following morning, she sensed something different in the air. Was it the cold and damp penetrating the very walls of the priory to reach her, or was this a feeling of foreboding, a bad omen?

All around her, her travelling companions and other pilgrims not known to her still lay asleep on their straw beds, but there was no sign of Humbert. The lower room of the hostelry was full and, as she had seen the evening before, the monks had even given shelter to pilgrims in the church of Saint Etienne itself.

The Untamed had slept fully clothed, and now she threw back the blanket that covered her, and quickly fastened up the cord of her breeches which she had undone for the night. Sitting on the edge of her straw mattress, she re-plaited her hair and then looked over her feet carefully. She had no actual wounds but was nevertheless pained by a number of blisters. Following instructions from the old *Jacquet*, she rubbed them gently with an unguent he had given her the day before; it was made with sage, elm and walnut-tree leaves. This done, she put on her knitted stockings and slipped her feet into her short leather boots. It was time to go and wash her hands and face.

There was a little trough dug out of the wall in the passage, which was intended for the pilgrims' ablutions. The priory at Aumont was scarcely a wealthy establishment, and had no steam room or lavatorium. The icy water made Bruna shiver, and she pulled her sheepskin-lined mantle round her more tightly. Seeing that her companions were still not stirring, she went out into the courtyard alone with a determined step.

The sun had not penetrated the clouds that morning, and the cold pierced her skin like a myriad evil little needles. The sky was a hard, metallic grey and it huddled down low like a ceiling, patched and flaking with wintry clouds. A strange fog hung just above the ground.

Humbert was up and ready, deep in conversation with the father hosteller. She went over to them, a little alarmed to see the men in such animated discussion at this hour.

'What is it, Humbert?' she asked, having bid good morning to the hosteller.

'We must leave, Bruna, and forthwith. Gather our companions together. The father hosteller has explained that this heavy laden sky is a sign that we can expect the *écir* at any moment and that this *nèfle* could soon rise up and block our route.'

'*Ecir*? *nèfle*? What do you mean, pray?' asked the young woman who had never heard such words.

'They are some of the dangers of this harsh country, the Untamed!' explained the hosteller. 'In these parts we have whirlwinds of snow not seen anywhere else, they are called the *écirs*. And the *nèfle* is this fog, which lies listlessly along the ground before rearing up and becoming so thick that a man can no longer see his own feet nor the friend who walks beside him!'

'I will fetch the others!' said Bruna, turning swiftly on her heel.

A few moments later, her mistress and the mason's family were ready. They had a frugal meal with the monks, and then set off at a good pace, leaving behind them the shelter of Aumont's fortified walls.

19

At first, all seemed to be well, as they made their way into the forest following the *via Agrippa*. On either side of the stone road stood the great trunks of beech trees. Their branches were laden with snow, and a heavy silence hung in the air. Even the birds made not a sound.

Bruna kept her eye on another group of pilgrims who had left Aumont at the same time as them, and who were rapidly drawing away from them up ahead. It was a group of some ten strong young men, very unlike Humbert's little group which was slowed down most notably by Bérengère. The mason's wife was having difficulty keeping up, and she was helped and encouraged alternately by her husband and her son. As for Bruna's companion, she walked with an almost inhuman regularity, always at the same speed, whatever the time of day and whatever the terrain, taking small even steps.

Ever since they had left Le Puy, Humbert had been walking just in front of Bruna, the two of them, each as sprightly as the other, liking their place at the head of the group. The old *Jacquet* set his group a demanding pace, and rarely even hesitated as to which path to take. He would sometimes stop to examine a wooden cross, the lichen on a tree or a particular stone, and then he would set off again, forging ahead like someone very sure of his way.

They had passed the Wolf Rock, a tall hill surrounded by the forest. Behind them, Bruna heard the distant echo of a marching song; another group of pilgrims would probably catch up with them soon.

At last they stopped at a group of houses which went by the name of Rieutort, and there they chewed on strips of dried meat and stale crusts of bread. While Humbert spoke to the local peasants, Bruna and Garin went to fill up the calabashes in the contorted stream which gave the village its name. Village was perhaps too big a word for these five long low houses with their thatched roofs.

'Bruna,' said Garin suddenly, 'do you think we will be stopped by brigands?'

The Untamed smiled.

'I sincerely hope not, Garin, but we shall see. Anyway, I believe we are too poor to be of any interest to them.'

'That is far from true, damsel!' said a voice that Bruna recognised instantly.

She turned sharply, almost dropping her calabash. It was the troubadour who had shared her room in the inn at Le Puy.

'Now, he looks different,' she thought. 'It's probably something to do with that beard that he is leaving to grow like most of the *Jacquets*; they can't shave because it is so cold. And he has such a strange way of staring at people!'

'You remember me, it seems! I did not know I'd made such an impression, gentle maiden,' said Ronan mockingly.

'Who are you and what do you want of her?' asked Garin, standing defiantly beside Bruna.

'Oh, but I see you have found yourself an attentive escort, although he looks a little young to defend you in times of trouble.'

The young man flushed with rage and was about to reply when Bruna laid her hand on his shoulder.

'It is nothing, Garin, this man is just a troubadour, someone who lies around in dingy inns and dusty market places!'

'Hardly a flattering introduction!' retorted Ronan. 'But I will make it my duty to change your mind, wild maiden of the mountains.'

'Strewth, I have no greater desire to have anything to do with you now, than I did in Le Puy! And besides, what are you doing here?'

'I'm following you, of course!' replied Ronan with aplomb. 'Because you have stolen something from me!'

'Me, stolen something from you?' cried Bruna. 'Oh, your wit does you credit, sire, you with the flat purse!'

'Cruel princess! Beautiful and proud as Makeba who stole the great King Solomon's heart!'

'I know your riddles, forsooth! Save them for girls with hearts as fickle as your own!'

Seeing the young woman's eyebrows furrowing into an indignant frown, Ronan swiftly added, 'Calm yourself, damsel, calm yourself, I am going sweetly on my way as you do and as do all these good people, I am going to Compostela.'

'You, a troubadour!' said Bruna who had scant respect for those lazy souls who spent their time singing.

'Fair damsel, you should know that troubadours are men like any other, and they may do their penance and make acts of faith like any other too.' And with these words, spoken with some emotion, Ronan turned and left abruptly. Goodness, that girl had the gift of making his blood boil!

When Humbert set off again, his group had joined up with Ronan's which consisted of Ronan himself and two sturdy townsmen. The troubadour, who had taken up the lead with the *Jacquet* and Bruna, sang vigorously:

> *'Errante voy, soy peregrino,*
> *como un extrano, voy en mi camino.*
> *Un nuevo peublo en marcha va lunchando aqui,*
> *por la esperanza de un ciudad de Dios que vendra!'*

> 'I am the pilgrim who goes his way a-wandering,
> like a foreigner, I follow my path.
> A new people walks on and struggles here,
> in the hope of attaining the city of the Lord!'

Humbert smiled and joined him in the song; it was one he liked well. The townsmen and Garin's father did the same, and Bruna surprised herself by repeating the words she did not really understand and which Ronan spoke with such passion. It was the first time she had heard him sing. He had one of those slightly hoarse voices that grips your very entrails and ties them in knots of emotion you cannot hope to comprehend.

As they walked on, forgetting their weariness as they sang, the countryside around them changed. The forest gradually disappeared, giving way to a vast white plain, dotted with huge blocks of grey granite.

20

They had just passed the bridge at Marchastel and two other pilgrims had joined them: a man who looked like a cleric and a young shepherd. Ronan was still singing and they all walked the faster for it, when they suddenly came face to face with a wall, or so at least it seemed to them. It was as if the fog had been waiting for them there, and it had formed an impenetrable mass to bar their route. As they stood and beheld it, it looked as solid as a wall of granite. Their singing dwindled and faltered; only Ronan sang on more quietly.

Then the wind freshened, a freezing wind bearing down from the north and carrying snow on its wings.

'You know this route, Humbert, what should we do?' asked Ronan, serious all of a sudden.

'We're in a difficult position,' replied the old *Jacquet*, his forehead beetling with concern, 'and we must act quickly, the *écir* is on its way. We could easily get lost in the fog, or even lose one another.'

'Let's tie ourselves together!' suggested Ronan. 'In the Orient when there are sand storms, that is what the Infidels do.'

Humbert smiled approvingly and replied with a hint of surprise, 'You are right, by my faith, Troubadour, I remember that.' And then he spoke out to the others, 'Does everyone have a belt, a rope or a strap of some sort?'

'Yes,' said Guillaume.

'We too,' said Bruna and the townsmen.

'Not I,' said the shepherd who had joined their group.

'Hold one end of your staff and give the other end to someone else.'

And so, tied and linked to each other, they set off again, penetrating ever further into the dense fog which hid them from view.

The snow had started to fall and, by some strange phenomenon, seemed to dance around them, wrapping them in its damp breath.

'The father hosteller was indeed not lying,' thought Bruna, bowing before the violence of the freezing blasts. 'Even where I come from, at Nérestang, I have never seen such whirlwinds of snow.'

The Untamed was holding the end of Humbert's strap, and pulling her companion behind her. Suddenly she bumped into the old *Jacquet* who had come to an abrupt stop.

'What is—'

'Silence, all of you!' scolded the old man.

They could hear only the moaning of the wind, a creaking sound and . . . something like running water. Bruna strained her ears. What she could hear was not the moaning of the wind – she was quite sure it was the groan of a fellow human being.

They were huddled close together in silence. They could feel some unseen threat hovering round them. Bérengère had to bite her hand to stop herself screaming. Bruna slowly took out her knife and waited, holding it firmly in her hand. She sensed that Ronan had done the same and had come to stand closer to her.

They could hear nothing but the roaring wind and the flowing water. Humbert had raised his stick and whispered to the troubadour who stood beside him, 'I must go and see. There is someone injured or dying. That sound was a person gasping for breath.'

Ronan held him back, putting a hand on his arm.

'Not you, Humbert! I shall go. You know the route. Without your help our group would be lost. Which way should I go?'

'Over there, I would say,' said the *Jacquet* holding his iron-tipped staff out to the right. 'That was where the sound came from. Be careful! If my memory serves me well, we are not far from the waterfall at Déroc. It flows off a tall cliff.'

'Do not fear, Humbert. What birds are heard calling in these parts?'

Humbert shook his head.

'You strike me as more of a man of war than of the rebec, Troubador. What is your name?'

'The one does not rule out the other. You yourself are more of a crusader than a *Jacquet*, I would say. Call me Ronan, that will suffice. So, which cry is it?'

'The white lady, and three times together,' replied Humbert.

'Very good.'

And the young man disappeared into the fog.

21

Humbert made them gather in a circle, putting the women – who had started to pray – in the middle. The men stood holding their iron-tipped sticks in both hands, their faces stony with tension, their ears straining for the least sound. The wind whipped their faces, but they paid it little heed. They stared steadily at the grey wall around them and, unable to see anything through it, they imagined the monsters and the dragons of their nightmares in its eerie depths.

Suddenly a stone rolled to their right. Humbert clenched his teeth, but then he heard a hooting sound, repeated three times. It was Ronan who emerged from the fog, but he was changed, his face ashen, his eyes aghast.

'What is it?' whispered Humbert.

'Come! There is nothing more we can do, but the others should not see this.'

'Stay in the circle and keep your eyes open,' instructed the *Jacquet* as he set off after the troubadour. When he tripped over the first body, he understood why Ronan was so overcome.

At his feet lay a decapitated corpse, and then another, and then yet another. It was a veritable massacre. The snow was red with spilt blood. There were almost a dozen slaughtered pilgrims there and in a flash Humbert recognised them. It was the group that had set off from the priory in Aumont at the same time as them. These men, whose strength and youth he had envied that very morning, had all been killed.

'Do you know them?' asked Ronan seeing the old man's horrified expression.

'They took shelter in the same place as us at Aumont.'

'We must have heard that one cry out as he passed away,' said Ronan, leaning over one of the pilgrim's bodies. 'His head was not cut off, he was stabbed in the side with a knife. It was probably the fog which stopped his assailants from finishing him off.'

'Let us go back to the others, Ronan. Whoever did this is probably not far away.'

When they arrived back, their companions' anxious faces all turned towards them. Humbert raised his hand to ask for silence and whispered, 'There is danger, my friends. There are brigands very close by. Our only safeguard is to remain silent and to take shelter in this fog.'

70

'What has happened?' the Untamed whispered in Ronan's ear. The young man's blue eyes looked the girl squarely in the face.

He said, 'You do me a great honour all of a sudden in choosing to speak to me. I shall only reply if you tell me your name, maiden.'

'I am Bruna the Untamed, you know that well!' muttered the girl heatedly. 'Tell me!'

'There's been an ambush,' said Ronan more seriously. 'Ten pilgrims have been killed, but don't repeat that. There is no point in frightening our fellow travellers.'

'Then why are you telling me?' asked the young woman, who had turned pale.

'I believe it would take much to frighten you, gentle Bruna,' said the troubadour, turning on his heel.

The little column carried on in silence. The roaring of the waterfall grew ever louder: it must be very close by now. Humbert was having trouble finding his bearings. Ever since they had set off again, he had felt as if he were going in circles.

At last the ground beneath their feet sounded different; he knelt down, swept away the snow with his hands and uncovered a large flat paving stone. They were back on the *via Agrippa*, back on the correct path. Unless . . . unless the brigands came back to exterminate them, too.

Humbert raised his hand and the little band froze. Within the roaring of the water there was another more urgent thundering: the hooves of many horses, heading straight for them.

'Stand back, stand back,' cried Humbert in alarm.

There was barely time. A deafening clatter filled the air. The frozen ground shook beneath their feet and suddenly, carving through the curtain of fog, more than a dozen horsemen appeared carrying long javelins. Their sturdy chargers were fitted with armour for war, with caparisons of leather, and metal masks to protect their muzzles.

Humbert gave a strange sigh and burst out laughing. Ronan looked at him in amazement: had he quite lost his mind? Then he turned to the horsemen who had come to a halt a few paces away, and he understood. All their swords were buckled, and over their hauberks they wore long surcoats bearing a blue cross with eight points.

'The knights of the Dome of Aubrac, Adalard's knights,' said Humbert, patting Ronan's shoulder. 'We are saved!'

22

Having listened to Humbert's account, the knights decided that it was more important to look after the living than the dead, and guided the pilgrims through the fog to the old fortified monastery known to all as the Dômerie of Aubrac.

They would deal with the brigands later.

The wandering band were coming closer to their goal and a deep, monotonous sound was carried to them, blending with the moaning of the wind.

'It is our bell ringing out to call us,' explained one of the knights who was walking alongside Ronan, having given up his horse to one of the women. 'When there are storms it rings without ceasing, day and night, it is the bell of the lost. Thanks to that bell, many a poor soul who has strayed from the path has been saved from the blizzards and the cold.'

At last they could make out the long low outline of the fortified walls through the thick fog. The knights headed towards a gate that stood wide open and was guarded by two men armed with javelins. The little group went through the gate into a huge courtyard. They had arrived.

The Dômerie at Aubrac comprised all in all two buildings of wood and granite, a bell tower, stables and an oven house.

'One of the buildings,' explained the knight, 'is an inn for travellers, the other a sanatorium.'

The travellers walked increasingly quickly as if afraid that this unexpected miracle of hospitality might melt away in the mist. Once the pilgrims were safely in the good hands of the brothers, the knights spurred on their chargers, turning them on their hocks and diving back into the snow and fog to find other lost pilgrims. They would only stop to rest once night had fallen.

At the door of the inn, a woman stood waiting for them with two serving girls. Although she wore a very simple kirtle of humble cloth embroidered with the same blue cross as the knights, everything about her indicated that she was of high birth.

'Welcome to the Dômerie,' she said with a slight bow. 'Are any of your number injured, my brothers?'

'Why no, Lady Amandine,' said Humbert, passing to the head of his companions and bowing very low before her.

'Another pilgrimage, my lord Humbert! I can see you grow stronger every time!'

'Pray, do not mock me, my lady, but may God heed your words! It is always a pleasure to see you again,' he added with a gallant flourish.

'Come in, come in! Your companions look quite frozen. How many are you in your party?'

'We have with us three women and we are eight men.'

The pilgrims went into a huge, vaulted kitchen, meagrely lit by a single tall narrow window. No place had ever looked warmer or more welcoming to Ronan and his travelling com-

73

panions. They looked about them with the almost dumbstruck stare of those close to exhaustion who have endured considerable suffering. A massive fireplace heated the room with tall, leaping flames. Torches were attached to the walls, and that one room seemed to them more lovely and more comfortable than a corner of Paradise itself.

A hearty smell of onions and gammon wafted from a large steaming cauldron above the fire. There were three pilgrims and a knight sitting eating at the long table, and they turned to greet the new arrivals with a nod before turning hungrily back to their bowls of soup. The two little serving girls led the group over to sit on the benches near the fire, and one of them gently took the little package that Bérengère held to her breast in her fierce grasp.

Then Lady Amandine came over to them, holding out a basin of hot water. She knelt before the mason's wife, took off her shoes and washed her feet with the warm water and then dried them with clean linen. The poor woman, her eyes half closed, was scarcely aware of what was happening, so tired was she.

Next it was Garin's turn. The young man opened his eyes wide with amazement, not daring to resist such humility and gentleness. Never, but never, could he have imagined that a beautiful woman, and a true lady, would wash his feet, as it was written in the Bible.

Another, older woman had come to join Amandine, and when they had washed all the travellers' feet, they invited them to come and lay down their belongings on their cots. A monk came by to take their dirtied mantles to have them cleaned.

A ladder took them up to the upper floor where there were two dorters for pilgrims and one for monks.

'We can put four of your companions in one of the rooms on the upper floor. The others will find room in the sanatorium. I will take the women with me. Three women making the pilgrimage, that is most rare,' Amandine said, turning to Bruna.

Feeling a little intimidated, the Untamed flushed and asked, 'Do you work here then, my lady?'

Lady Amandine smiled kindly.

'Yes, young damsel, in the upper room of the sanatorium we have ladies' rooms. We are three ladies who live here and serve our Saviour in the form of his pilgrims. But, tell me, what is the matter with your companion, my child? Is she not well in herself or is she injured?'

Lady Amandine's practised eye had picked up on the strange bearing of the woman who stood beside the Untamed.

'Indeed not, my lady. She is always thus. That is why she has undertaken this pilgrimage,' replied Bruna.

'What is her name?' asked Lady Amandine gently.

Bruna opened her mouth but did not speak.

'Has she no name, then?'

'Why yes, my lady. Her name is Lady Freissinge,' whispered Bruna. 'Lady Freissinge of Apchon.'

Lady Amandine came closer and gently pushed back the hood that hid the woman's features. The torches lit up a delicate face and a little bun of braided brown hair. It was a face carved in translucent wax, a face in which nothing moved, not even the eyes with their tiny black pupils.

Bruna hurriedly lowered the hood.

'Forgive me, my lady,' she said, 'but I must ask you not to.'

Lady Amandine frowned; she looked at Bruna and whispered, 'You must speak to me, damsel. This woman seems to me to be possessed by something. Such a burden seems a heavy one indeed for shoulders as tender as yours. And you intend to take her all the way to Compostela like this?'

'I gave my word on it to my master!' announced Bruna.

'Do you know that it is hard enough to make this journey successfully alone, damsel? But in this case it is as if you were carrying a childling. She would not be able to look after herself if any harm came to you.'

'I know all this, my lady, but I shall be strong and our Saviour will help me.'

Lady Amandine looked at the Untamed's small, determined face and said, 'Strength is not everything, young damsel, and with a woman like this you will have to watch out for her more carefully than you would for yourself. But I do not wish to make you lose faith, I believe that you will keep your word, come what may.' Then she turned to the old *Jacquet* and said, 'My lord Humbert, as you know our house well, take three of your companions to the sanatorium. There is still some room near the chapel. Meanwhile, we shall prepare the platters for you to sup.'

'Many thanks, my lady!'

'My sister Isabelle will lead you, my ladies,' said Amandine. 'If you wish to change your clothes you may . . . and I recommend it. She will take your shifts and breeches, and will lend you clean tunics to wear. Tomorrow we will give you back your own clothes as good as new.'

Bruna went over to Amandine and took her hands, squeezing them in her own with passionate gratitude, before turning away with tears in her eyes. Ronan, who had watched the exchange went over to Humbert.

'I will come with you to the sanatorium, if that does not trouble you.'

'Not at all, quite the contrary. And Guillaume and Garin shall come with us too.'

The mason and his son nodded their agreement.

Their faces were still blue with cold and their hair still trickled with melting ice, but the sparkle in their eyes had been rekindled. Their weariness had melted away like the terrible snows in the heat of that safe haven.

23

Old Humbert liked this place well.

'I feel at home here, and I think that I could end my life here, if God and the abbot Dom Guiral would have me,' he explained to Ronan.

He was taking his companions to the sanatorium, as familiarly as though he had only left it the day before, stopping on the way to show them the stables, the oven and the little postern in the fortified wall. Then he pushed open a heavy door and let his companions pass.

The vaulted hall of the sanatorium was divided into three huge rooms. One was a dorter which could accommodate some fifteen patients, and was separated from the chapel by a little balustrade of sculpted wood. Next to it was a smaller room reserved for knights and clerics. In the other part there was a kitchen with a roaring fire and a wash house where the pilgrims' dirty clothes were soaking.

Ronan, who often criticised the wealth of churches, found more beauty in this Dômerie than in any other sacred place. And yet, what austerity! Everything here was done for the service of pilgrims and to ensure a sparse survival in this place which so deserved its name of Aubrac, *alto bracum*, meaning a high place where man was not welcomed by the elements, especially in the harsh, dark winter months.

The chapel, which the ailing could see from their very cots, held no furniture at all. It had only a slab of granite by way of an altar, a cool block of grey rock with the tiny dancing flame of an oil lamp upon it. On the walls hung a large wooden cross with eight points, the symbol of the knights of the Dome.

Isabelle showed the women to the upper floor. There were eight cells reserved for the seriously ill and the infirm, as well as the ladies' rooms and a room for the Dom of Aubrac, the abbot of the Dome.

Since the death in 1135 of the Flemish viscount Adalard, who had founded the Dômerie, this assembly of high-born ladies, of monks and of knights had appointed the young Brother Guiral to succeed him and lead their little community. Dom Guiral was a man of science and of letters, and he spent his days serving pilgrims and his knights and tending the sick or studying. He had heard the chargers' whinnies in the courtyard and had come out of his room to greet the new arrivals. With his strong square face and close-cropped blond hair this man of God had the appearance and the vigour of a man of war, but these characteristics were belied by the eternally gentle expression in his eyes.

He welcomed Humbert with a wide smile as if he had only left the day before, and greeted the four men warmly. Then, seeing the women, he bowed respectfully before them.

'What a pleasure it is to see women pilgrims in this place,' he said. 'Please treat our premises as if they were your home, my friends and, before God, we are your servants.'

24

Ronan remembered that night for a long time.

The dorter was full. Humbert, the mason and his son all slept close by, and all around them lay pilgrims delirious with fever, shocked, injured or so exhausted that they lay as inert as the dead in their simple beds.

Night had not yet fallen before Ronan had sunk into a deep sleep. Then he woke with a start. He had heard the clatter of hooves and whinnying . . . the knights had come home. After having a hasty meal in the kitchen, they came into the chapel to pray before making for their dorter.

Ronan went back to sleep gazing at the little flame flickering on the altar. From time to time a moan or one of the patients calling out would draw him from his slumbers. Then the silent figure of a monk would run over, passing from one bed to another, handing out unguents and potions.

Above him, Ronan could imagine Dom Guiral bent over his unintelligible scribblings and, further over, the ladies' room. Would the Untamed be asleep, strange creature that she was? He smiled. He felt well in himself, as if he were at home – home, what a strange word for one such as he to use, he the wanderer, the rootless.

And the night drifted past.

25

A grey dawn had risen. After Mass, the *Jacquets* had gone into the frater. There was still some soup and some bread. Their shifts and mantles were clean and still warm from the hearth where they had dried as best they could.

Now they had to set off and leave this place free for the others who would come after them. When the Dômerie was out of sight, the pilgrims felt heavy-hearted as if they had each left their own home as, in some small measure, they had.

What they did not know was that they had also left behind them the mutilated body of a young novice, lying buried under a pile of snow at the foot of the fortified walls.

PART THREE

26

While he waited for the messenger to return from Saint-Alban, the Baron de Peyre champed impatiently at the bit. Galeran, for his part, was haunted by the Moor woman's premonition, and his imagination dwelt on it far too much for his own liking.

To pass the time, the ageing lord had invited him to join him in a game of chess. The two men sat facing each other before the great chimney of the lower hall. A squire had brought them the chessboard and laid out the painted pieces upon it. Like many warriors, the baron had a fondness for this game which had been brought back from the Orient by the first Crusade. He had initiated a goodly number of his trusty followers in the game, and they took pleasure in coming to challenge his prowess. Indeed, he threw himself into the game with the same furious energy he deployed on the battlefield, massacring as many pieces as he could before encircling the enemy king in one corner of the board, and rising to his feet with a cry of triumph.

Galeran, imperturbable as ever, never took his eyes off the chessboard. After a while, he deliberately sacrificed a bishop and, taking advantage of the baron's astonishment, attacked with his castle and his knight. Checkmate was inevitable, and the elderly lord, who was loath to lose in jousting or in chess, furrowed his brows in apparent anger.

'I can accept such a speedy defeat only at your hands, Chevalier,' he said with an arrogant tilt of the chin.

'There is no question of defeat, my lord, just a heated exchange, and it is a pleasure crossing swords with you.'

A servant hurried into the room, interrupting this bitter-sweet verbal jousting.

'The messenger has returned, my lord, and my lord Baudri has arrived and is asking to see you.'

'Send for the messenger first. I will receive Baudri once I have seen him.'

The man's face was blue from his speeding ride through the cold, and he bowed promptly before the baron.

'Alas, my lord, I bring you little news. As you asked, I went to Saint-Alban and also spurred my horse on all the way to La Chaze. No one alerted me to any disappearance, even in the houses several leagues from the toll.'

'Which is as good as saying that we know no more now than we did before!' growled the baron, his eyes gleaming angrily. He dismissed the messenger with a curt flick of his hand, then turned to the chevalier who had remained silent during the brief exchange.

'By my life!' he cried, 'I am sorely vexed by this, and I know neither what to think nor what to do. What think you, Galeran, you who are well versed in this sort of enigma?'

'For my part,' replied the chevalier, 'I am almost certain that the boy who died at Estrets was from among the pilgrims, was indeed a pilgrim himself! And Marchastel is also on the *Jacquets'* route. That is a coincidence no one can deny.'

'Yes, but why on my land, Galeran? Am I being singled out in some way? Some act of vengeance against my person?'

The chevalier shook his head.

'I think not, Baron . . . unless you are hiding something from me.'

'By my troth, I am not,' rejoined the baron heatedly, 'you have seen me as I am, I would not know how to lie!' He thumped his fist down onto the chessboard, scattering the

84

pieces onto the flagstones. 'But, in the name of all that is holy, what is this new evil spewed from the mouth of hell?'

The chevalier gave no reply. His gaze lingered on the bishop which had rolled to his feet and now, its wooden face cleft in two by the fall, lay staring at him balefully.

'A madman,' whispered Galeran, 'or some creature with two faces like this broken chess piece.'

'My lord Baudri,' announced a squire, stepping aside to let an elderly knight into the room. The man wore a full-length travelling mantle splattered with mud and melting snow.

The baron's face lit up when he saw him.

'Ah, Baudri, my cousin, what a pleasure to see you again.'

The knight knelt before the baron who lifted him back to his feet and embraced him heartily.

'Galeran de Lesneven, Breton knight, in whom I have put my trust,' said the baron introducing his guest. When the two men had greeted each other, a servant drew up another chair and the three men sat down by the fire.

'It is not often, Baudri, that you appear before me in such a state. You are still in your travelling mantle, did you not realise?' teased the baron.

Baudri started in surprise and leapt to his feet, throwing his mantle to his squire. His face never lost its serious expression.

'My lord Baron, as you know I have come straight from Le Puy where I attended the Pascal Mass.'

'Yes, I know of your great friendship for Bishop Pierre III, and the care that you take not to miss his services. But that is surely not what lends you such an anxious expression?'

'Indeed not. I left the City of the Virgin the day after the great pilgrims' departure. Everyone at the bishop's palace could talk of only two things, two very grave matters.'

'Tell us, then, tell us!' exclaimed the baron who was already growing impatient.

'Two bodies were found, my lord. Bodies which are making things very difficult for the bishop's men, particularly the second.'

'Who was it?'

'The first one is known because his companions have identified the body. He is a lord from the Auxerre region.'

'A young man?'

'Indeed not, a mature man.'

'How did he die?' asked Galeran.

'His throat was cut clean across. It was probably the work of thieves because his purse and his seal had been taken.'

'And the other?'

'The other was a boy of about fifteen, he was found along the ramparts in the Saint-Jacques area.'

'His body was just one huge wound, so often had he been stabbed, his tongue and his noble parts had been sliced off, had they not?' asked Galeran gently.

'How do you know this?' Baudri asked in astonishment.

'Two men have died on my land,' barked the elderly baron, not giving the chevalier time to reply. 'Two deaths of this kind, served up in the same hideous way. Oh, Galeran, Galeran, indeed you were right!'

'I stopped in Marchastel . . . you mean that the shepherd who was found . . .' Baudri said slowly.

'Yes,' replied the baron sharply.

27

Galeran had excused himself, leaving the two men to matters concerning their estates. He was sorely troubled and inaction weighed heavy on him. He could not simply wait calmly while other murders might be committed: he had to act.

Once he was in his bedchamber he sat down on the edge of the cot, delved through his leather saddlebag and took out a wax tablet and stylus. He had been using this method for writing things down – so favoured by monks sworn to a vow of silence – for several years. The waxed surface allowed him to set down his ideas clearly and to unburden his mind of the bustling details which might become clues and then proof once they were engraved into the smooth white wax. Then he would erase everything by warming the wax so that it remained a virgin surface until his next investigation.

First of all Galeran put down the name Le Puy Sainte-Marie, then Estrets and Marchastel: three places, three bodies. The prediction was coming true, there was indeed blood on the white path to Compostela, there was a killer following the 'milky way'.

The stylus sank further into the soft surface: now Galeran was drawing a labyrinth with Compostela, the field of stars, at its centre.

'He is hiding among the penitents, and what better hiding place than this great body of unarmed men travelling towards Galicia! Only, how to find him? The only clues he is leaving us at the moment are the bodies marking out his route.'

Judging by the time that had elapsed between the various

murders, Galeran guessed that this monster was killing regularly as he carried on along the way like the pilgrims. But had he attached himself to a group of faithful travellers or was he walking alone? There would be advantages and inconveniences in both instances. Within a group he would attract less attention, but his attitudes and behaviour might alert his travelling companions. On his own, he would be more difficult to catch, but he would also find it more difficult to gain the trust of the pilgrims he met.

With one furious gash of the stylus, the chevalier struck out the names engraved in the wax. He could not still the rage in his heart, not only rage but – possibly for the first time – a feeling of powerlessness. The Moor woman's words rang fatalistically in his ears again: '. . . they died, and you could do nothing to save them.'

This particular chess game was being played out on a giant chessboard, a chessboard the size of a kingdom, a chessboard on which, at least for now, the murderer had taken the upper hand, eliminating pieces with the chilling regularity of a methodical player.

The baron had told him that the *via Agrippa* took the pilgrims to Aubrac. That was where he must go, and the sooner the better, because he sensed that this killer was unlikely to slacken in his slaughtering: he took too much pleasure in it.

Galeran wrapped his wax tablet and stylus in a linen cloth and bundled them hurriedly back into his saddlebag. He took off his doublet, and put on his hauberk and a sturdy leather capuchon to protect him from the snow and the wind. Then, picking up the last of his belongings, he hitched up the clasp at the front of his mantle and took up his weapons.

The baron did not move when he heard the chevalier's footsteps. His cousin Baudri had left and he was alone, pressing his foreheat against the lintel of the chimney, watching the dancing flames.

Without even turning round he said, 'I knew you were going to leave, Galeran. I cannot come with you, there are matters that need my attention here. But I do have many trustworthy men. Would you like them with you?'

'No, Baron, armed men would only serve to alert our game. But I know not the *Jacquets'* route. Is there someone among your people who might take me as far as Aubrac or even beyond?'

'Indeed yes, I have thought of that, I have sent for old Jaufré. He has much to commend him. He is from Nasbinals in Aubrac, and can take you there with his eyes closed, and that might prove to be very useful because the plateau at Aubrac is often bathed in fog and snow at this time of year. His second asset, and the better of the two, is that Jaufré was once a *Jacquet*. He made the pilgrimage when his wife died, but he came back to me afterwards. He will be of great help to you, he is a good man.'

'But will he still be able to make this terrible journey?'

'I said that he was old, but do not trouble yourself, Chevalier. He is stronger than an oak tree, believe me. I have asked for your horse to be readied and for provisions to be prepared. I shall give Jaufré one of my own chargers, so that he does not slow you down.'

'How can I thank you, Baron?'

'Thank me not, Chevalier. It is I who am indebted to you for helping me to keep my word. Catch that creature from hell and ensure your own safe return!'

28

Since they had left the rocky outcrop of Le Peyre, followed by the echoing horns of the watchmen, the two men had ridden on in silence. The fog was now nothing but a bluish mist underlining the horizon and the snow had ceased to fall.

The baron had been truthful, the former *Jacquet* knew the way well. They had cut across the woods to Marchastel, then the two men had launched their steeds onto the *via Agrippa*, making up much time. The baron's charger was a powerful animal whose stride was well matched to Quolibet's, Galeran's trusty gelding.

From time to time, the two horsemen would pass slow-moving groups of pilgrims, and they would slow their horses to a walk to pass them, before spurring the animals on again. Galeran did not truly know what he was looking for. He would linger to study the *Jacquets'* weary faces before speeding on to catch up with Jaufré who had carried on ahead.

Jaufré was an archer and he carried the signs of his trade: a warrior's bow lay across his back, and a quiver full of arrows hung from his shoulder. Like most archers, he wore a short, fur-lined tunic and had a fur-edged leather hood to protect his head. He had a leather glove on his right hand and his left forearm was protected by a fine plate of iron.

As they rode along the chevalier had explained to him the purpose of their journey, and had neither hidden from him what sort of investigation this was nor what danger there might be in accompanying him. Jaufré, who was a far from talkative man, had nodded his head without breathing a word, a thoughtful expression on his lined face.

Much later, as they approached the lands of the Dômerie, he had made this simple statement, 'We will find him and you will kill him, my lord.'

Galeran had nodded. This elderly companion of so few words suited him well.

They had left the forests behind them and were now riding across a white plain strewn with huge blocks of granite. The north wind had started gusting across the plain making it icy cold. The horses had been forced to slow their pace as their hooves sank into a thick carpet of powdery snow which threatened to trip them at any moment.

The mournful ringing of a bell was carried to them on the wind. Jaufré pointed towards the distant view of a walled settlement with granite buildings huddled under their snow-covered roofs.

'That's the Dômerie, and what you can hear is Maria, the Bell of the Lost.'

Quolibet, Galeran's charger, whinnied nervously and shook his mane.

The chevalier patted his old companion's neck to steady him; he too had sensed something strange, a muffled thudding which made the ground vibrate. He turned and saw a whirlwind of snow bearing down on them at great speed. It was armed horsemen galloping towards the Dômerie. There must have been twenty of them and over their hauberks they all wore white mantles and the Templars' cross.

Quolibet pranced nervously and the chevalier understood why when he saw that the Templars were driving with them about a hundred wild horses. The animals hurtled down the slope in a hellish clatter of hooves, and no good would have come to any man or beast that stood in their path.

'Where are these Templars from?' asked Galeran. 'I knew not that there was a commandership in these parts.'

'Oh, it is not truthfully a commandership. They have a small fort at Recoules. They breed horses there, and that is all.'

The old archer watched the horsemen who hollered and whooped to drive the horses towards the far end of the plateau. He pointed out the direction in which they were heading to Galeran and said, 'The Dômerie is at a meeting of the ways, I do not think that they will stop there. They are making too good a headway. You see, they are going on past it. And anyway, they scarce see eye to eye with Dom Guiral's knights. These are men of war, whereas the knights of the Dômerie are devoted to pilgrims and to the poor.'

'And where are they heading with those horses?'

'Over that way is the road that the *Jacquets* take, but over there, the direction in which the horsemen are heading – do you see? – that road goes straight towards Sauveterre and the Cévennes. The Templars are heading for Anduze or La Couvertoirade. From there, they will take their horses towards Spain or the Holy Land.'

Jaufré fell silent and the two men spurred their horses on to reach the Dômerie.

When they entered through the fortified wall they were greeted by the most tremendous commotion. The knights of the Dômerie were most displeased by the Templars' passage over their lands, but that was not what had vexed them the most.

A monk came over to the new arrivals and greeted them. He was pale and seemed preoccupied.

'Good day to you, sires, what can we do for you?'

'We are sent by the Baron de Peyre, and I should like to meet your abbot, Dom Guiral,' replied the chevalier dismounting and handing his reins to Jaufré.

'I have to tell you that we have been touched by a great misdeed, and Dom Guiral is in the chapel—'

'What has happened?' asked Galeran, his throat tightening as he thought he could guess the answer.

'When one of our brothers went to empty a bucket of slops outside the walls he found the body of one of our novices under the snow – But, this is our business, or at least it is Dom Guiral's.'

'Tell Dom Guiral that I can probably shed some light on this death, if he consents to see me.'

'What are you saying?'

'Go and simply tell him what I have told you. But be quick. Every moment is precious,' Galeran said insistently.

The monk stared at the chevalier and what he saw seemed to convince him, because he turned on his heel and sped off towards the sanatorium. Meanwhile the old archer had taken care of the horses, rubbing them down and leading them to the water trough before leaving them to eat the hay that a stableboy had brought for them. When he came back over to the chevalier, Galeran indicated that he should stay in the yard and keep a discreet eye on the comings and goings of the pilgrims.

29

That particular morning Dom Guiral did not have his usual serene bearing. His high forehead was cut in two by an anxious furrow, and an angry light glowed in his black eyes. He came straight over to the chevalier and greeted him.

'If you can help me, my lord, please do so, this is a very serious situation.'

Galeran shook his head.

'It is you who shall help me, Dom Guiral. I am tracking a beast hiding in a man's body, but I know not what he looks like. Was your novice tortured with knife wounds and were his tongue and his parts sliced off?'

'Yes,' replied the abbot bitterly.

'Could I see him, and then could I speak to you in a quiet place?'

The abbot nodded and gestured for the chevalier to follow him:

'Come, my lord.'

After examining the body, which lay on a litter near the chapel, the two men went up into the abbot's private quarters. Dom Guiral paced anxiously up and down his cell as if he had quite forgotten his guest. Galeran remained silent, and stood motionless in the doorway, waiting for him to regain his composure.

At last Dom Guiral indicated a chair to Galeran and he himself fell heavily onto a stool.

'Forgive me, Chevalier the sight of this poor innocent creature tortured to death is more than I can bear. I am listening.'

'Did you see him alive yesterday?'

'Yes, and he carried out his work as usual, his companions have confirmed that to me.'

'Where did he live?'

'In the hostelry, in a communal room with the brothers. I have already spoken to the monks. The man next to him in the dorter saw him rise and go out alone. He thought that he must be going out for a nocturnal call of nature. Then the brother simply went back to sleep.'

Galeran was overcome by a strange feeling of excitement. He could scarce believe his ears and was almost unable to contain himself. Did not the unfortunate novice's death prove that the killer was still in the Dômerie as recently as the night before – or in the area at least. In short, in easy reach! Suddenly, the scope

94

of the enquiry – which, just the night before, had seemed almost limitless – had been dramatically reduced.

'Do you know the pilgrims who stayed here last night, Monsignor Abbot, and who left this morning?' asked the chevalier feverishly.

'Well, there were two groups that left us this morning. One of them was found in a snowstorm by my knights last night. They were a group which included three woman pilgrims, a very rare thing. Yes, that's right, there were ten or eleven of them in all, I know not. But we knew one of their number well, he has made the pilgrimage three times already, it is my lord Humbert, a good man.'

'What were they like? Could you describe them to me, Monsignor. I will have to recognise them.'

'Oh, well, as far as Humbert is concerned, that's easy, but I can assure you that he is not your man. He is not tall, he has white hair and a white beard which he wears plaited, he has a big old faded blue mantle with his three shells stitched to it.'

'Did you know the pilgrims who travelled with him?'

'No, but that is not all. Three of the ailing in our care left shortly after them.'

'Had they been here long?'

'About five days.'

'And in what way were they ailing?'

'One was dying of hunger; another, like quite a few of the *Jacquets*, had decided to make the journey barefoot and he was nearly dying of the cold as a result of it; the third, I know not, he was in a sort of stupor, probably due to exhaustion. As they were recovering, they set off again for Compostela. I think they wanted to catch up with Humbert's group.'

'Did Humbert seem to be on very close terms with his travelling companions?'

The abbot thought for a while.

'I did not see them much, I had work to do in my cell. Wait, I shall call for Lady Amandine. It was she who took them in. Will you excuse me?'

'But of course, please,' said Galeran and he thought to himself: 'Eleven or fourteen suspects. It is becoming more manageable than the original two thousand! He must be among those people, unless he stayed behind here, but something tells me that he did not, that he moved on, as he has before.'

Dom Guiral returned, making way for a woman who, like the knights of the Dome, wore the blue cross on her long kirtle. She was simply dressed, and a few wisps of blonde hair escaped from under her head-wrap to set off her pleasing face. Galeran noticed the alert intelligence in her blue eyes as they scrutinised him. The woman greeted him and introduced herself in a gentle voice, 'Chevalier, I am Lady Amandine, at your service.'

Galeran bowed over her proffered hand.

'Galeran de Lesneven, Breton knight and friend of the Baron de Peyre. I am most grateful to you, my lady, for troubling to see me so quickly, as, in truth, time is short.'

'Dom Guiral has explained to me why you are here among us, Chevalier, it is my duty to help you. I cannot bear to imagine others being tortured and killed in the same way as our poor novice. Ask me your questions, and I shall answer as best I can.'

'Thank you, my lady. I need to know about the people who arrived with my lord Humbert.'

'Yes. First of all there were three women. Well, to be precise, there was a mason with his wife, Bérengère was her name, and their son, a young man of about seventeen. Then there were two other women pilgrims. The first was a young girl who came from the Auvergne mountains, or that is what she told me. A good, strong girl who wore breeches like a man. Very black hair and high cheekbones, a bit of a gypsy girl to look at. She was accompanying a woman who, by my faith, was quite without her wits.'

'What are you saying? What do you mean by that, my lady?'

'Young Bruna was making the pilgrimage on her master's request, and was taking this lady to Compostela that her reason might be restored to her, or that was what the girl led me to understand.'

'Do you not believe her, then?'

'I admit that the woman did make me feel uneasy.'

'Bruna?' asked the chevalier.

'No, her strange mistress . . . Lady Freissinge, if my memory serves me well.'

'Lady Freissinge?'

'Yes, the lady . . . how can I explain it? I have already seen people who have turned their backs on the world, but it seemed to me that she was consumed by something disturbing. I could not say what. I tried to warn the young girl but she would not hear me. Her companions called her the Untamed and, upon my word, it becomes her well.'

'Who were the others?' asked Galeran.

'I did not spend so much time with them as with the women, who slept in our room, but there was a troubadour who stayed with old Humbert. After the meal I saw him sitting by the fire cleaning his rebec before going up to his cot.'

'What did he look like?'

'A fine face, with brown hair and a beard, an olive complexion and very blue eyes, rather like yours.'

Lady Amandine frowned and looked more closely at the chevalier.

'But, now that I think on it, this man was really very like you. Yes, except that he must have been older than you.'

Galeran shuddered as a feeling of foreboding swept over him.

'Do you know his name, my lady?'

97

'I heard it, but I remember it not. We see so many people, new people every day.'

'Was his name Ronan?' asked Galeran.

Lady Amandine shook her handsome head.

'Forgive me, Chevalier, try as I might, I cannot remember his name.'

'I see a man of your lineage. He is in great danger,' the Moor woman had said. Could it be that Ronan, his elder brother, was among the pilgrims? wondered Galeran. The errant Ronan caught up in a group of pilgrims and walking alongside a murderer.

But what would he be doing there, he who was supposed to have left for the Orient never to return? No, he must be mistaken. This accursed prophecy truly was becoming an obsession.

Galeran went on in a calm voice:

'And the others, my lady, could you describe them to me?'

'As I said, I know only Humbert well, and I believe the abbot has already described him to you.'

'And who else was with him?'

'Four men who slept in the hostelry. Two of them seemed like wealthy townspeople, judging by their clothes.'

'Can you think of anything in particular about either of them?'

'Nay, in all honesty, I cannot.'

'Who else?'

'A young cleric, or that was what he looked like. He read before going to his cot, but I did not see what it was he was reading. And another man, dressed like a shepherd with a surcoat that was lined with sheepskin and a large leather pouch. He was young too.'

'You can think of nothing else, nothing at all? Think carefully,' insisted the chevalier.

Lady Amandine struggled visibly to recall any small detail.

'The shepherd, yes, the shepherd,' she said suddenly. 'He had a scar on his foot. I saw it when I washed them. It was like a bite mark all the way round the ankle. No, not so much a bite, it was more like a rope mark: as if a rope had dug into him.'

'Lady Amandine, one last thing, you said that the women slept with you?'

'Yes, that is so, in this very building, in our room which is next to the abbot's own chamber.'

'You also said that the four men slept in the hostelry. And the others? The mason and his son, the troubadour and Humbert, where did they sleep?'

'Here, I believe, in the sanatorium. Yes, that was it. They were given places over near the chapel, where you went earlier.'

'Many thanks to you, my lady.'

'Have I helped in some small measure?'

'Indeed you have, without a doubt,' replied the chevalier as he turned towards the abbot.

'You may go, Lady Amandine,' said Dom Guiral gently.

When she had left Galeran said, 'Dom Guiral, may I ask you one last service? I would like to visit each and every one of the ailing staying with you.'

'Do you think . . . do you think it possible that the man we are seeking is still here?'

'I do not think so, but I wish to neglect no possibility, Monsignor Abbot.'

30

Jaufré reined in his mount and drew to a halt before a stone pillar engraved with an eight-pointed star.

'We are leaving Dom Guiral's estates, my lord Galeran.'

The chevalier looked around. In these parts the Aubrac plateau was quite devoid of trees, and the low-lying mist was only punctuated here and there by outcrops of grey granite.

'Tell me, Jaufré, how long would it take us to catch up with a group that left the Dômerie this morning?'

'It is not as simple as that.' The old archer sighed. 'There is not just one road to Compostela, but a dozen.'

'What do you mean?'

'From here some people follow the *via Agrippa*, but you told me that they had an experienced *Jacquet* leading them. Now, such a man might choose to stay on the Roman road or to cut through the woods at Aunac to get to the Olt gorges near Espalian.'

'What do you think, Jaufré?'

The old man shook his head gloomily.

'I have made the journey only once, my lord.'

Galeran's charger whinnied nervously and the chevalier stroked him soothingly while he thought.

'Right, given that it will be difficult to find them, let us overtake them. What is the next major staging post for the pilgrims, somewhere that they all stop?'

'At Conques, my lord.'

'How long would it take us to get there?'

'It is a long way off and the road will not be easy for our

mounts. The gorges are very steep, we will have to walk and lead our horses.'

'Be that as it may, how many leagues are we from Conques?'

'As far as I can remember, some twenty leagues.'

The chevalier frowned.

'Night is falling quickly, we shall, therefore, not be there today, but towards the end of the day tomorrow, if we sleep little and drive our horses hard.'

'Yes, God willing, it would be possible,' agreed the old archer.

'Good, we shall wait for them there, then. Onwards, onwards, Jaufré, and may God help us,' said Galeran, spurring on his charger.

31

Jaufré had guessed well. A few leagues further on the group of pilgrims lead by Humbert had indeed crossed through the woods at Saint-Chély and stopped at Sainte-Côme d'Olt. Bérengère was exhausted and, as it was already mid-afternoon, Humbert had decided that it would be wisest to stop for the night. He was not, however, rewarded for this sage decision: the hospice was full to the rafters and there was not even a single lowly mattress left free in private homes. Luckily, Humbert remembered once long ago being put up in a farm some little distance away and he took his companions there.

Night was just beginning to fall as they emerged from a wood of sweet chestnuts and saw, about half a league away, a stoutly constructed building with a high wall of granite surrounding the farmyard and cowsheds. The door to the enclosure was closed and the pilgrims were greeted by the furious barking of several dogs on the other side of the wall.

Humbert struck the door firmly with his staff and the barking redoubled. Eventually, the door creaked open on its hinges and an elderly woman appeared in the doorway gazing at them open-mouthed. The old *Jacquet* greeted her with great courtesy.

'God keep you, my good woman! We come in peace. We are pilgrims travelling to Compostela. If you recall, you gave me board and lodging some years back, and I am still indebted to you for your kindness.'

The woman screwed up her eyes and her expression softened.

'That may well be true, by my faith! But how many are you? There are women among you by the looks of it!' she said, raising herself up to look over the rest of the group.

'Yes, there are eleven of us,' replied Humbert. Then, seeing the old woman's expression, he added, 'But we can pay for a little soup and some bread, if you have any to spare.'

The woman hesitated, before eventually agreeing. A few coins never went amiss and this man spoke the truth.

'My husband is in Sainte-Côme with our boys, they'll be home soon. In the meantime you can set yourselves up in the animal sheds. You will find plenty of forage there to make beds, it is perfectly clean. As for a meal, I'll go and see what I can do.' Then she brought her face right up to Humbert's and said, 'I know you, that's for sure! I remember now although I don't see so clearly. Will you be answerable for the others?'

'Yes, good woman, I will ensure that we will not cause you any inconvenience, and we will leave tomorrow morning at milking time because we have a long way to go.'

'Very good, very good. You, at least, are a true *Jacquet*, I can see that. But these days there are so many vagabonds around.' Then she removed the heavy chains that held the door closed and added, 'Don't worry about the dogs, they're tied up!'

As she allowed them in she launched into a long discourse about the 'bad sorts' who came past begging and passing themselves off as *Jacquets* when they were nothing but scoundrels. Humbert nodded: she was quite right. Over the last few years he had met a good many of these frauds who wore shells on their mantles, even though they had never undertaken the pilgrimage!

'There you are!' said the woman, pushing open the door to the animal sheds. 'Make yourselves comfortable in here, but don't upset my animals and don't start any fires!'

Inside was an enclosure full of sheep and goats which started bleating as the pilgrims came in. The peasant woman had been as good as her word: the animals leant the place a most welcome warmth, and over behind a wooden partition, away from the slurry, the sweet-smelling hay was piled high.

Once the door was closed behind them they all laid down their belongings with obvious relief. They were totally exhausted and numb with cold. The mason's wife crumpled onto a hay bale, and Humbert came over and sat down next to her. He was concerned about her condition. They had not yet covered one quarter of the journey, and the old man could scarce see how she would cope with the trials that lay ahead.

'How do you feel, Bérengère?' he asked kindly.

'Not very well, my lord Humbert, I am so wearied and so cold,' she replied through chattering teeth.

The *Jacquet* looked at her attentively and lay the palm of his hand on her forehead: she was burning with fever and her eyes were gleaming with tears.

'It's nothing. You are a little fevered, Bérengère. Once we have made an agreement with the farmer, I will warm some wine with herbs that I carry with me in my pouch for you. After a good night's rest, the fever will pass.'

The mason, who had followed this conversation between

Humbert and his wife, came over to him as soon as he stood up. His face looked strained and he asked numbly, 'How do you think she is, my lord?'

'All will be well, my friend, indeed it must!' replied Humbert. 'Just make sure that she is very well covered this night. I shall give her a potion which will cause her to sweat copiously and tomorrow, God willing, she will be recovered. A little weak still, perhaps, but recovered.'

Guillaume nodded gravely.

'I wish I could believe you . . . Oh, sire, I have so many regrets for having dragged her all this way with me. But, you see, we no longer had any choice . . . We could either die of hunger at home or die on the journey, what's the difference, sire? Tell me that. The only difference is the forgiveness of sins, is it not?'

32

At the far end of the shed the forage was piled right up to the rafters. There were chestnuts drying on long racks, and young Garin eyed them longingly.

'Holà, Humbert,' said the young man slipping down beside his friend. 'So, can we settle ourselves here?'

'Indeed yes, make yourself a bed, my boy. We shall have a hot meal again this evening.' Humbert added with a sterner note, 'As for those chestnuts, stop thinking about them. You don't want to be mistaken for a common thief, do you?'

Garin flushed and stammered, 'It's just they're so beautiful, and there are so few of them where I come from. And, truth to tell, my belly is quite hollow!'

The old *Jacquet* turned away from him with a stern tilt of the head, and Garin did not see the thin smile which spread across his face.

Not far from them, Ronan was tuning his rebec as he spoke to the cleric and the two townsmen. He had thrown his scanty belongings on top of a pile of hay and seemed in no hurry to go and rest.

As for Bruna, she had covered Lady Freissinge with her mantle. The latter had huddled herself beneath it and seemed to be asleep. The Untamed briefly caught the eye of the old *Jacquet*, and turned away uneasily.

The door opened and a blast of cold air swept through the barn. Two strong men came in carrying a heavy pot full of boiling water. A boy followed them with two tallow lanterns. On their instructions, Humbert and Ronan put a flat stone down on the ground for them to put down their heavy load.

The two men stood up and the older of the two took a pouch from over his shoulder.

'Welcome to our smallholding, my lord *Jacquet*. I do remember you. My wife was right. She made this for you and your fellow companions,' he said, opening the bag to show him boiled chestnuts and hunks of bread rubbed with lard.

'Will you thank her for us? And our thanks to you,' replied Humbert, taking the bag. 'What can I give you in exchange for all this?'

'You'll have to agree with her in the morning,' grumbled the farmer. 'Money matters are for the wife. If you pray for us, she won't make you pay so much, though!'

'We will pray for you as we have this meal, my friend, and in Compostela too, before Saint Jacques's tomb. Could I come and warm up a remedy by your fire, one of my pilgrims is unwell?'

The man glanced briefly over towards Bérengère, nodded and turned to leave.

'Yes, surely, but be quick. It's been a long, hard day and we shall be putting our feet on the forewood early this night, my wife and I.'

The child put the two tallow lanterns down on the ground before leaving behind his father.

Ronan took the pouch from Humbert and said, 'Go on, Humbert. We will get everything ready here. Don't take too long, with the cold, this water won't stay hot for long.'

'What's the "forewood"?' Garin asked the shepherd who had sat down next to him behind some bales of hay. The young man looked at him with an amused twinkle in his eyes.

'Oh,' he said with a shrug, 'I think it must be part of their bed. They step onto it to get to bed, so putting their feet on the forewood is like going to your cot!'

'Do you know these parts then?' Garin asked, looking at the young man with amazement.

The shepherd could only have been in his twenties and looked more like a childer than a man who worked on the land. Even though his shoulders were broad he had a narrow waist, and his fine, regular features were framed by blond curls. Only his hands, with their callused palms and broken nails, betrayed his harsh lifestyle.

'Oh, shepherds travel a wide area. And in places like this there are caravans of mules all the way from Spain bringing olive oil, spices and cloth, and people like myself often follow them back south, even as far as Galicia, to hire out our strong arms.'

'Why then are you making this pilgrimage if you've already been to the far side of the mountains?' asked Garin.

'I'm not really making it,' said the other confidentially. He had a soft almost feminine voice, but his cold, calculating eyes reflected his hard character.

'What do you mean, you're not really doing it?'

'Well, I'm travelling with you, but I'm not going all the way to Santiago, I'm stopping before that.' The shepherd puffed himself up slightly as he added, 'I have a very good friend in Galicia, you see . . . a woman, and I'm going to join her there. I gave her my word on it last year.'

'You're going all this way on foot to see a girl!'

'Well, I suppose so, yes, but she's not a girl!' replied the other with a shrug of his shoulders. 'A widow, and a rich one! She is an ugly wench, but she's taken quite a liking to me. She promised me that if I came back she would marry me.'

'And do you trust her to keep her word?'

'Oh, indeed yes!' said the handsome shepherd with an angry shake of his blond curls. 'I worked for her a year ago, and showed her that I was a man.'

Garin opened his eyes wide.

'You mean that you took her?'

'Zounds, indeed yes! And how! So you see, I'm going back, and we are to be married. I'll give her many children, and I'll oversee the shepherds who come to me for work.'

'I would not care to go with an ugly woman!' exclaimed Garin.

'Zounds, I am not of a mind with you! Whatever women are like, it's always easier to get on with a man, don't you think?'

As he spoke, he had laid his strong hand on the young man's thigh and was eyeing him insistently. Garin was so taken aback that he was quite speechless. Then, as the other man's hand worked its way further up his thigh, he leapt to his feet, strode over the bales of hay and went back to join his father.

'Fie, fie, you are too young to understand!' The shepherd sighed, getting to his feet.

33

Only the flickering of the tallow lanterns now remained to light the circle of *Jacquets* round the cooling pot of water. After a fervent prayer, each had filled their bowls with the soup of bread and chestnuts and had sat eating in silence.

'Penitents or men of faith, guilty or innocent, children of hell or children of heaven, who knows?' thought old Humbert as he contemplated the circle of faces reduced to tragic masks by their weariness. It mattered little, in the end. Over the years he had learned to walk quite at his ease amidst these nomadic ghosts, and he had renounced the urge to discover their intimate secrets.

Once they had all finished their meal he announced, 'My companions, it is nearly ten days since we left Le Puy Sainte-Marie.' Their exhausted faces turned towards him. The time had come to instil new faith and hope in them, to tell them about their goal which was drawing closer every day. 'In three days we shall reach the beautiful town of Conques and we will have finished one of the most demanding parts of our journey.'

'But I've heard quite the opposite, that the hardest part is in Iberia, my lord Humbert. The mountain crossing kills many a pilgrim, even without the wild beasts and the bandits marauding in that desolate country!'

The cleric's words were met with icy silence. He did not seem to notice it, he had lowered his head and seemed lost in sad thoughts.

'Indeed not!' protested Humbert. 'The mountain crossing and the Roncevaux pass will be difficult, there is no denying that, but we can hope for more clement weather, and the rest is just a question of perseverance and faith in God.'

The cleric did not react. Beside him the other *Jacquets* looked gloomy and despondent. All they could see before them were the leagues and leagues they needed to travel and the manifold dangers they were likely to encounter.

Ronan, who had listened attentively to this exchange, watched the cleric carefully and wondered what terrible sin this ascetic man was atoning for as he obstinately insisted on making this pilgrimage barefoot through the snow. Although he was extraordinarily thin, he was far from ugly. One might even be tempted to say, if he were not so stooped and huddled in the cold, that he had presence. No, what was disturbing about him was the look in his cool, distant grey eyes, and his indifference to everything around him. Even the day before in the worst of the blizzard on the Aubrac plateau, he had stood with his arms crossed, undaunted by the danger that threatened them all. He was a strange man and, all along the way, he probably only tolerated the others' company because they were necessary to his own survival.

Ronan shrugged his shoulders. There he was judging a man whose distaste for the whole world could only compare favourably with his own. Besides, what did he have to teach to anyone, now that, once again, he had forsaken the quill and the rebec for iron and spilt blood? He had set off to the Orient to find his fortune. He had travelled all the way to Tripoli, at last finding peace in the company of an old man, a disciple of Omar Khayyam. He had smoked hemp, written quatrains and honoured the red rose of womanhood every day and every night, then . . .

The troubadour shuddered. As if through a fog, he heard Humbert's voice still speaking. He was here and now, he was in this barn in the depths of the Olt region, and not on a terrace in

109

Tripoli looking out to the dark-blue sea.

The old *Jacquet* stood in the middle of the pilgrims telling them the legend of Saint Jacques and the milky way. Garin was sitting at his feet, his eyes shining and his mouth open in wonderment. Humbert knew the white path, and the faith that burned through his words lit a fire in the eyes of the men and women around him.

When he had finished his tale, the old man caught his breath before saying in a calmer voice, 'Fellow *Jacquets*, it would be good if we are to continue on this route together for us to learn a little bit about each other. We have already faced dangers together and we do not even know each other's qualities. I think it is time we got to know each other better. I myself, God willing, will be your guide all the way to Santiago de Compostela. My name is Humbert, former crusader and experienced *Jacquet*.'

'Ronan of Brittany, *trouveur* and traveller, my lords,' said Ronan in turn.

'Guillaume the mason, and this is Garin and my wife's name is Bérengère. We come from the county of Blois.'

'Miss Bruna and Lady Freissinge from the mountains of the Auvergne,' said the Untamed hastily.

'I am Manier the shepherd, happy to be among you!' exclaimed the tousle-headed shepherd with the steely eye.

'Master Pierre, goldsmith from Le Puy Sainte-Marie,' said one of the wealthy-looking townsmen.

'Master Raoul, a weaver. I come from Lyon.'

'My name is Arastaigne,' uttered the cleric grudgingly.

'Hey!' exclaimed Ronan. 'But that's a name from my part of the world! Where is it that you are from, my lord Arastaigne?'

The cleric seemed to hesitate, then replied icily, 'I have turned my back on the world and the world has turned its back on me. What does it matter where I am from?'

110

'You are right, it matters little where we are from, because all the matters is where we are going, is that not so, Humbert?'

The old *Jacquet* nodded his approval. 'Yes, that is indeed true. And soon we shall see Compostela, for God is with us! He has protected us thus far and, by my faith, he shall continue to do so.'

The faces lit up around him, Humbert's fervour had erased their exhaustion and discouragement.

'And now, my companions, I think you should sleep. The days to come will be gruelling and we will need all our strength to reach Conques.'

Everyone dispersed, looking for some corner to make themselves comfortable. Ronan's gaze lingered for a moment on Bruna as she huddled herself in her mantle before lying down at her mistress's feet; then he shrugged his shoulders, laughing at himself. He settled himself as comfortably as possible between two bales of straw and closed his eyes.

The wind whistled in the rafters. From time to time a plaintive bleating rose from the herd of animals and, suddenly, sleep overwhelmed him.

34

The two horsemen had had to spur their horses on to reach Conques before nightfall. They had managed to cover the ground in two days, and felt pleased to have done so in such harsh conditions.

Their chargers breathed heavily and their coats were splattered white with foam. Galeran raised his hand, indicating that Jaufré should stop beside him. Beneath them a walled town complete with ramparts emerged from the beech woods, clinging to the side of the mountain. The light of the setting sun flashed off every shiny surface including the river which wound its way along the floor of the valley.

The chevalier turned to the old archer.

'That is Conques and the Abbey of Sainte-Foy, my lord,' said Jaufré pointing out the twin towers of a large church. 'Below it is the river Dourdou. The pilgrims will take that bridge over there in the distance when they set off from here towards Figeac and Cahors.'

'Do you know anywhere that we might be given bed and board, and stabling for our steeds, Jaufré?'

'Indeed yes. One of my countrywomen will put us up. She lives near the Vinzelle gate, and we can put the horses into the barn next door.'

'Come on then, Jaufré. A good meal and a sound cot are just what we need!' Galeran called out behind him as he coaxed Quolibet on again with a kick of his heels.

Soon the two horsemen came out onto a narrow paved path, lined by low drystone walls, which led straight to the ramparts of the fortified town. They dismounted, mingling with the groups of pilgrims passing through the Fumouze gate.

As they arrived inside the town they saw a spring of clear water rising straight from the rock itself into a stone basin. There were children filling calabashes and offering them to the pilgrims with welcoming smiles. Benedictine monks showed the *Jacquets* over to the hostelry or the basilica, carrying the sick and the injured on stretchers.

The two horsemen had trouble forcing their way through the throng in these narrow streets known as *carriérous*, so full were they with tradesmen's stalls and money-changers with their ledgers. Everything here was at an angle, and, according to

Jaufré, the square in front of the abbey was about the only part of the town that was level. The people of Conques even joked that you went into their houses through the attic and came out through the cellar!

The snow had well and truly melted, and here and there a slate roof gleamed silver in the dying light. Compline Mass had not yet been rung in when the two companions reached the narrow cob house in one of the tiny *carriérous* near Vinzelle, the shoemaker's district.

While Galeran held the two horses, Jaufré climbed up the three steps and knocked at the door. An old woman opened the door and froze in surprise when she saw who had come to see her. Then a wide smile lit up her round face. She briskly wiped her hands on her plain tunic and cried, 'Well I never, Jaufré, my friend, how good it is to see you again! What good timing, I have not finished eating. But you are not alone?'

'No, Marguerite,' replied the archer. 'May I introduce Chevalier Galeran de Lesneven? We are travelling towards Compostela.'

'Right. Wait for me here. I'm coming back. My grandson's here. He'll take your horses to the barn next door before he goes home.'

The old woman hurried indoors and came back out with a young man who twisted his smock shyly as he greeted the two men.

'Rub them down well,' said Galeran, patting Quolibet's steaming neck. 'They've earned a good rest, they've served us bravely.'

'Indeed I shall, my lord!' said the boy, taking the horses by the bridle.

'Come in, come in!' cried the old woman. 'There's still some hot soup and some sweetmeats just as you like them, my old Jaufré.'

In front of this comely, curvy woman, 'my' Jaufré had shed several years and Galeran could not help himself smiling to see his old companion flush scarlet. Marguerite took them over to a large table in front of a brazier. It was warm and dark and full of good smells, a mixture of garlic, bread and honey.

She sat down commandingly on a large stool and gestured for them to do the same. Despite her age, she looked like a big, beautiful, rosy apple. She smiled at them as she served the soup for them, not even asking why they were there but acting as if this were quite normal and she was perfectly accustomed to seeing them.

The archer laid his hand on her arm and whispered hesitantly, 'Thank you, Marguerite. You haven't changed at all, you know.'

'Oh, don't start, Jaufré, you're not going to woo me at your age!' said the old woman with a wicked twinkle in her periwinkle-blue eyes.

Before the curfew was rung in Marguerite led them to a tidy little room that she used for storage. She put down two straw mattresses and withdrew, wishing them a good night.

'Well, well,' said Galeran good-naturedly, 'that's the sort of hospitality that I like. Your friend Marguerite is as fine and dependable as a good loaf of bread!'

'She was my sweetheart, my lord. She was from Aubrac, like myself. But I was young and restless; I set off with my bow and a quiver full of arrows to conquer the world. When I returned ten years later, she'd given in to the charms of a shoemaker from Conques, a good man, I have to say. When I made the pilgrimage after my wife's death, I found Marguerite here by chance. She had been widowed and I realised that she still had a place in my heart.'

Jaufré fell silent and the chevalier respected this silence, moved by his simple story. He took off his mantle and laid it on a cask before lying down on his mattress. He wrapped himself in the thick blanket Marguerite had given him and said quietly, 'We must get to sleep early and gather our strength, Jaufré, because the time has now come to stalk our game more closely.'

'What are your orders, my lord Chevalier?' asked the archer, waking from his thoughts.

'We will take up posts. You will be by the Plô fountain to keep watch over the entrance to the abbey enclosure. I shall stay on the inside, not far from Sainte Foy. An old *Jacquet* such as Humbert will not fail to come and pay homage to the town's patron saint.'

The archer looked troubled.

'But how shall we find them among so many pilgrims, my lord?'

'Remember, Jaufré. An old *Jacquet* with three shells on his mantle, three women, a troubadour . . . somehow or other we shall flush them out.'

The archer nodded in silence, wrapped himself in his blanket and turned towards the wall. Like all old soldiers on the eve of battle, he went straight to sleep and was soon snoring loudly.

The road outside was still bustling and noisy but this gradually died down in the still of the night. Galeran was left alone with his thoughts, remembering the face of the young shepherd boy and then that of the novice; but in the forefront of his mind danced the dark, foreboding face of the Moor woman. He, who had not believed her prediction, was now beginning to think that her tragic eyes could have been a thousand years old, and that she knew the future as well as he knew the ways of the sword.

35

They had been there for two days and still nothing. They had seen scores and scores of pilgrims pass, pilgrims of every age and description. Sometimes there were so many people in the town at once that the priests held their Masses simultaneously in all seven chapels round the chancel.

At nightfall when the basilica showed no sign of emptying, Galeran and the archer took turns to observe the reliquary. They hid in the shadows beside the strange statue of the saint which was covered in gold and precious stones, and which gleamed serenely, fixing them with its enamelled eyes.

There were dozens of people clustered round her every evening, and, despite their exhaustion, they sang psalms to the little martyr who had died before the Roman Emperor Diocletian when she was only twelve years old.

The afternoon was drawing to a close, and Galeran thought it was about time to see whether Jaufré had any news. He went out into the paved courtyard and stopped under the tympanum depicting the final judgement, grateful for the warmth of the last few rays of sunlight. All round him, pilgrims gasped and commented on the sculptures representing the demons and the damned. One of their number, a young man with staring eyes, could not tear himself away from the image of a devil biting off the head of a damned soul who was stabbing himself in the neck to escape the devil's clutches.

Galeran turned away. Jaufré was over by the Plô fountain. In order to reach him he had to cross the square in front of the

116

basilica, which was no mean feat at this time of day. In the evenings, hoards of pilgrims gathered here for a few moment's relaxation, sacrificing a few precious coins to the bear-handlers, the acrobats and the troubadours.

The chevalier made his way through the crowds, just missing bumping into a juggler so skilled that the balls he juggled seemed to have a life of their own. It was then that he heard a voice over the hubbub, a voice he thought he recognised, a voice that stirred so many memories in his mind that his face froze. He carried on as best he could and eventually reached the singer.

The man was wearing a long cape, he had brown hair and wore a beard, and he accompanied his song with the plaintive lilt of a rebec. When he had finished, he bowed to the cheering crowd and they threw him a goodly amount of money, for there was in his voice that husky resonance which inflames men's passions and troubles women's hearts.

The troubadour picked up the coins and stood up again, and came face to face with the chevalier. He paled and stood rooted to the spot. They stood like that for a long time, looking at each other. Then the chevalier took the other man in his arms.

'Ronan! How good it is to see you again.'

The troubadour pulled away from his embrace and took a step back.

'Greetings, little brother,' he said breezily. 'I did not think to see you here. God is indeed good to grant me this joy. You have not changed or, rather, you have, you look more and more like the blade that you wear by your side!'

'What are you doing here? Are you going to Compostela?'

'Yes, I'm making the pilgrimage and I shall reach the end, God willing, little brother.'

'Are you travelling alone?'

'Indeed not, on the contrary, I have several good and helpful

117

travelling companions. But come with me, be my guest. I have a few *deniers* now for us to treat ourselves. There is a roast-house near here, a tavern where they roast fine meats. What better place to celebrate our reunion!'

Galeran agreed a little uneasily.

'Yes, yes, as you wish, Ronan. But wait for me here a while, I must let the man I am travelling with know.'

The chevalier hurried off, dogged by dark thoughts. So Ronan was back and it was indeed he who had been to the Dômerie. But, when all was said and done, who was Ronan? There was a big age gap between the two brothers, and when Ronan had set off for distant lands to find his fortune, Galeran had been scarce more than a childling. And then there had been silence . . . a silence of nearly ten years during which, judging by the evidence, providence had smiled little on the young adventurer, slowly turning him into this man, aged prematurely and begging for a few coins in the square. And yet he had lost none of his pride, and still spoke to his younger brother with the same condescending tone which used to annoy him so! No, Galeran sighed, as far as he could remember, they had never really seen eye to eye.

36

Trusty Jaufré was standing by the fountain, and his face lit up when he saw the chevalier.

'So?' he asked. 'Still nothing? We might as well try milking a billy goat!'

'Quite the contrary. I think we have something at last, but I have to make sure,' said Galeran, and he briefly explained the situation to the archer. 'My good Jaufré, there is no need for you to keep watch tonight. Go back to Mistress Marguerite. I shall join you before the curfew. Go and check on the horses, we shall have to be on the road again at dawn tomorrow. Make sure the tack is ready.'

'Very good, my lord,' said the archer with enthusiasm; the inactivity had weighed heavily on him.

When Galeran re-joined his brother he found him deep in conversation with a dark-haired girl dressed in the trappings of a pilgrim.

'Galeran, may I introduce damsel Bruna. She comes from the mountains of the Auvergne and is travelling in the same group as myself.'

The chevalier scrutinised the young woman and remembered the description given by Lady Amandine at the Dômerie: 'A good, strong girl . . . very black hair and high cheekbones, a bit of a gypsy girl to look at.' He bowed, sensing that she felt uneasy under such close scrutiny.

'Forgive me, damsel. But it is so rare to meet a woman making the pilgrimage that I forgot simple manners. My name is Galeran de Lesneven.'

'And are you . . . are you Ronan's brother?' she asked a little sharply.

'I am his younger brother. Ronan is the eldest in my family, damsel,' said the chevalier with a little smile.

Bruna bit her lip, turned to Ronan and asked spiritedly, 'So, you are happy to deceive everyone, just like that! Are you really a man of the sword, not of the rebec?'

'Is it so important to you then, damsel, to know which instrument I can play?'

Bruna flushed to the roots of her hair and cried, 'Oh, you . . . you. . . !' and turned on her heel without even bidding the two men goodbye.

Galeran burst out laughing and slapped his brother on the back.

'Good and useful travelling companion, as you were saying. Rather well put together your travelling companion, I would say!'

'Indeed yes, but what a filthy character to go with it!'

'In any event, she is doing everything she can to hate you, but it looks as if she is far from succeeding.'

Ronan shrugged and his face darkened a little before he said, 'Come on, little brother, let us go and drink. We have so much to tell each other. It has been such a long time, nearly ten years, since we have seen each other.'

37

When they were sitting down facing each other with their pitchers of wine, however, they were perfectly silent. They suddenly realised that they had become complete strangers and each one probably had secrets he could never admit to the other.

Watching his brother closely, Galeran weighed up the pros and cons. In the end he decided that this unexpected reunion could help him with his enquiry. Laying aside his doubts, he told the troubadour candidly about the whole affair. When he had finished, Ronan drank deeply from his wine before saying mockingly, 'Is that really it, little brother, or is there something else you want to tell me?'

'Why? Are you frightened?' retorted the chevalier, who was already needled and angry.

'No, but put yourself in my shoes! You're saying that I have happily travelled all this way with one – or possibly several – abominable criminals; that I have shared my bread and my prayers with them without even realising it?'

Galeran smiled.

'And why not? What do you know about them? They are all just casual acquaintances, are they not?'

Ronan was quiet now, his brow furrowed with concern.

'What are you expecting me to do?' he said eventually.

'To introduce me to your *Jacquets* as your brother, because there is no need to lie. And I will set off for Compostela with you.'

'But your archer, your horses, your harness? You cannot make this journey like that.'

'Jaufré will go ahead or follow up behind with my horse and harness. Your companions must not even know he exists. I have no intention of raising the assassin's suspicions.'

'I accept,' said Ronan, patting his brother's shoulder. 'In any event, it will give us an opportunity to spend time together and, if this beast truly is among us, I will help you track it down!'

38

Oil lamps were being lit along the little streets of Conques, and the tradesmen were beginning to take down their stalls. A powerful young man stood out amidst the bustle of the pilgrims. He was of noble birth and wore fine clothes, his long sword knocked rhythmically against his feet. He was obviously hoping to find some damsel to make him a happier man, and he eyed them all covetously.

A few moments earlier he had left his companions in one of the roast-houses, promising to return in time for the curfew. As he walked, he thought about the penitence that Abbot Aurillac had given him. He had been given orders to go to Conques and to join the pilgrims travelling to Compostela.

Now he was wondering with some amusement whether God would mind too much that he had come on horseback, surrounded by his cheery companions, rather than barefoot and alone. But, at twenty-five, most men believe themselves to be immortal, and they fear neither the Lord nor the Devil.

The man was black-haired and hot-blooded. It was in fact because of this hot blood that he had killed a nobleman on the square in front of the church of Saint Géraud in Aurillac, an act which had obviously not been to the taste of the abbot. And all this because when Robert was not making war, making love and talking about it were his principal pleasures . . . after hunting. In fact, he thought, the two were very much alike.

But now, Robert was becoming impatient. For two days he had been seeking a girl to pleasure, and not one woman had given him more than a smile or a sideways glance. It seemed that this was a time for praying, not for the delights of the flesh. Of course there were brothels and prostitutes, but he had never had to resort to their services, and thought he was far too young to have to pay for his carnal pleasures.

Where he came from, in the Aurillac region, the wives and daughters of peasants were proud to give themselves to him, and if they would have none of him, he took them anyway. After all, according to his numerous conquests he was a good lover, and he did not believe in keeping this talent to himself. When he made them scream it was with satisfaction and not for the lack of it. As for girls of high birth, he had already spent many a happy hour with compliant young virgins of good family, and even if he did not always achieve his aim, very few pretty girls refused to go bathing with him and show him what they hid from everyone else.

Just as he was thinking of giving up and returning to his companions he saw her. Wrapped in a long mantle, she walked alone and apparently aimlessly through the streets, buffeted by the streams of pilgrims. He was experienced in this particular kind of hunt, and could imagine her fine face and body under the hood and thick cloth of her mantle. Catching sight of her as she was jostled by a passer-by he even glimpsed a pretty profile and fine, curving eyelashes.

He decided to follow her and, catching up with her, took hold of her shoulder before she could escape into the crowd. He was expecting her to show some sign of surprise, but she simply turned towards him and he let his hand drop from her shoulder. She had lifted the hood of her mantle slightly from her face, and they looked at each other intently.

The woman's eyes were only half open and they seemed to be veiled by a strange impenetrable mist, as if she did not even see him, and her skin was so pale it looked like virgin snow. He would not have been able to say why she had such an effect on him. She was scarcely beautiful. She was simply very unusual. She reminded him of the elusive reflection of the moon in the half light at dusk or dawn . . . and of other things too, to which he could not even put a name. All he knew was that this particular woman made his blood burn hotter than any other.

Pulling himself together, he bowed to her, not wishing to alarm her.

'Forgive my audacity, damsel, I thought you were lost and . . .'

Still she said nothing and stared at him so insistently that he felt uncomfortable. This particular hunt was not running the same course as the others. He felt the woman's gaze roaming from his long ermine-edged cape to his madder doublet and then resting on his long sword which almost swept the ground.

At last she turned away, and continued on her way as calmly as if he had never existed.

'Ah no, my lovely, wait for me!' he roared, hurtling after her.

He soon caught up with her and blocked her way with great self-assurance. She stopped, but the expression on her face did not alter one flicker.

'Do not be afraid, damsel, you have not given me time to introduce myself. I am Robert d'Aurillac, at your service.'

The woman still did not react.

The young nobleman hesitated. Should he abandon all hope of a conquest? His pride told him not to. On the other hand, for the first time in his life, he did not know how to behave with a woman. That was when he realised that he still had not heard her voice. She must be afraid. He took a few steps back to show himself off to best advantage, putting his hand onto the handle of his sword to give himself added presence.

'If you do not wish for my protection, damsel, speak. Otherwise—'

Before he could make another move, she had slipped away into a tiny side street and disappeared.

The street was so narrow that a man of stout frame would have had trouble passing along it. Apart from a few tiny basement windows protected by strong bars the walls were blind and featureless, and dripped with saltpetre. The place was used as a urinary more than a passageway.

Robert hesitated, then his pride won him over and he ran after her into the alley. He could make out her outline in the shadows. She was not even running. To cap it all she stopped and turned, unclasped the front of her mantle and let it fall to the ground, revealing a long kirtle held at the waist by a red leather belt. Then she took her two long plaits and began to unravel them slowly, as if she were in the privacy of her own chamber.

Robert had frozen on the spot; he was so close to her that he could have touched the lustrous hair that fell in heavy curls. No longer able to contain himself, he grabbed the woman and drew her to him. A peppery smell emanated from her body and Robert felt the blood beating in his temples so powerful was his desire to possess her.

'By my faith,' he muttered, standing back a little the better to look at her, 'are you a nymph or a witch?'

She gave no reply, then took a few steps back before running further off along the dark alley.

'Accursed woman!' he wailed, throwing himself after her. 'Stop provoking. Do you want me to put you at my mercy?'

That was when he saw the glint of the blade as it came down. A searing pain tore through his chest. He closed his eyes against the intensity of pain. He felt that he had been struck again, again and again, and he knew that he was going to die.

39

It was a beautiful morning and the streets of Conques were now empty of all the pilgrims. They had started out on their journey at dawn, great streams of them, and Galeran had been among them.

As for the old archer, he had bid his farewells to Marguerite and, as he made his way to the barn where the horses were stabled, he struggled on with his dark thoughts. For once he did not agree with the chevalier. The latter had asked him to wait for him at Cahors, and Jaufré thought that this rendezvous point was too far away. On horseback he could be there in a day, or perhaps two if the going was difficult and if Galeran's gelding slowed him up by pulling against the lead rope. The pilgrims, on the other hand, would take six or seven days to reach Cahors, and this time lapse might allow the assassin to strike again while the archer would not be there to help the chevalier.

This was what Jaufré was thinking as he passed by the tower at Vinzelle and ran into a troop of armed men carrying a stretcher covered with a sheet. The sergeant heading up the sinister cortège stopped dead and stared at the archer before crying out, 'Jaufré, my friend, is it you?'

The archer shook himself out of his reverie and looked at the man in front of him. Despite the sergeant's age, he still had a proud bearing and, like Jaufré, he wore a large bow and a quiver full of arrows with blue fletchings. If Jaufré did not truly recognise the bearded face, he did remember the bow and the colour of the arrows. He came up to the sergeant and slapped him amicably on the arm.

'Bernart . . . but I thought you had set up home in my country, in Aubrac?'

'Well, no. You see, after all our battles, I found work here in Conques. And there is plenty of work, believe you me, with all these so-called pilgrims: the pilferers and the beggars. But fie, I have a goodly home, I am well fed, I am well paid, and at our age . . .'

'At our age! Our age! Oh, I see you haven't changed!' exclaimed Jaufré with a wide smile. 'Always complaining and always busy with something!'

'Yes, but sometimes,' Bernart added more seriously, 'I'd rather be doing a different job to this one.'

'Because of . . . ?' asked Jaufré indicating the stretcher.

'Indeed yes.'

'Show me.'

'It's a pretty piece of work,' said Bernart, lifting the sheet. 'Hacked about with a knife like a piece of roast meat. By the

126

looks of his clothes, he was a knight. But he had no money and no jewels left on him when we found him. It's funny, though, that they didn't take his boots or his weapons.'

Jaufré looked at the body's ashen face. He had been a good-looking man with thick black hair. The rich madder-coloured brocade of his doublet was torn in several places revealing clean wounds that still oozed dark, congealing blood.

'He isn't wearing very much for this time of year, your knight, is he?' Jaufré commented. 'His doublet isn't even fur-lined and did he not have a mantle?'

'I think it was taken.'

'Or he was killed indoors, that would explain his light clothing.'

'I hadn't thought of that, but, my goodness, you're right, my friend. Of few words, but well-chosen ones, like in the good old days. I'll repay you for that some day,' said Bernart, pulling the cover back over the body.

Jaufré sighed. He was at least relieved that this one had died thus rather than been mutilated like the others.

'And you, my Jaufré,' asked the sergeant after a few moments of thoughtful silence, 'are you living here or just passing through?'

'I am leaving this very day.'

'Shame! Duty calls, as they say!' grumbled Bernart. 'I'll have to leave you now. God keep you, my friend. And if you can, come back to Conques, we'll surely find the time to empty a few pitchers between us like old times!'

Moved by his words, Jaufré nodded his consent and gave his old brother-in-arms a last friendly cuff on the arm. Then he stood motionless for a good while, watching the sinister cortège moving off up the steep little street, scattering frightened passers-by who signed themselves with the cross at the sight of it.

PART FOUR

What you teach, so you should do,
and what you do, so you should teach.

Preface to Theodulfe's Bible,

eighth century

(Le Puy-en-Velay)

40

It was cold and the air was filled with the sound of the pilgrims' laboured breathing as they lay sleeping, huddled against each other on the floor of the cave. The chevalier woke, his senses bristling; he could hear footsteps and twigs cracking outside. The feeble morning sun filtered onto the outlines of the *Jacquets* sleeping round him.

Ronan lay beside him, his face buried in his hood, sleeping peacefully. The only person missing was Humbert. Perhaps he had preferred to sleep outside under the stars. The chevalier smiled, if he knew the old *Jacquet* he was probably already busying himself around the fire.

Galeran rubbed his arms and legs which had stiffened in the cold and damp of the night, then he put on his boots and stood up without a sound. Once outside, he stretched and looked round as he fastened his belt on which his sword hung. From where he stood he had a panoramic view of the surrounding area.

It was going to be a lovely day and the fresh air outside was a relief after the stifling atmosphere of the cave with its saltpetred walls. A golden mist smudged the blue of the sky, and the grass twinkled under a fine layer of rime. He looked down towards the town of Carjac, cradled in a circle of cliffs, and beyond it to the bridge they would use to cross the Lot river.

Humbert had hunkered down by the embers of the fire and was coaxing them into life, throwing on the dried twigs that he had put to one side the night before.

'God's blessings on you, Chevalier,' said the old man without turning round. 'Did you have a good night?'

'Very good, Humbert. But you are an exceedingly early riser,' replied the young man sitting down beside the *Jacquet*.

'I have little liking for the damp, it does nothing to help my aches and pains. And at my age I no longer sleep much anyway. Neither do you, it seems,' he commented with a malicious glint in his eyes. 'In the four days since we left Conques you seem to have slept with only one eye closed!'

The chevalier smiled and ran his hand over the beginnings of a beard.

'Quite so, Humbert. But we are both men of war, you know as well as I that sleep can lead to more than just dreams! I will go and fetch water from the source,' he added, rising to his feet.

'Why yes. I have a little lard and garlic left. Bérengère will need something hot this morning. The others too, I should think.'

'I heard her coughing in the night,' said Galeran. 'A bad cough. Has she been like this for some time?'

'Since Aubrac. I did tend to her, but her constitution is fragile and she has gone downhill again. Truth to tell, I am much afeared that she will not stay the course.'

'Why not leave her safely in a sanatorium so that she can regain her strength?'

'I have already suggested that, of course. But she insists that she does not want to leave her family, she is as stubborn as an ass! And, unlike us, Guillaume's family will not be returning from Galicia.'

'Do they want to settle along the *camino francés*?'

'Indeed yes. Many are tempted to do so, it is a chance to have a parcel of land at a goodly price and a guarantee of work. Especially as the husband and the son are both masons.'

'I have some knowledge of medicine, and I could try to tend to her at our next stopping point,' offered the chevalier.

'We must never lose hope, but the poor woman could easily die on the journey like so many others if . . .' The old *Jacquet* fell silent, weariness etched across his heavily lined face. Galeran turned away discreetly and picked up the empty aquamanile which lay on the ground beside him.

'Chevalier!' Humbert called him back.

'Yes?'

'May I ask you a question?'

'Indeed you may, Humbert, but I may not be able to answer.'

Old Humbert gave him a penetrating stare.

'That would be my loss, then. Tell me, Chevalier, it seems that you are very interested in us – in our group. You speak to each of us, or rather you make each of us speak to you – why?'

Galeran hesitated and then announced gravely, 'I would tell you a lie if I were to reply now, Humbert.'

'You are not here for the pilgrimage, then, nor even for your brother,' said the old man calmly.

The chevalier smiled and raised his hands to ask for peace.

'Hey, hey, Humbert, give me some respite, I beg you, and judge me not so quickly. I shall speak on all this again when we are in Cahors, if you so wish.'

The old man nodded and said, 'I shall make a point of it, Chevalier!'

41

Having followed the course of the Lot river, they climbed up towards the plateau at Salvagnac and toiled under the harsh white light reflected by the limestone. All along the route there were little walls and shelters formed by the rock; Humbert called them *garriottes*, which meant little houses.

A group of pilgrims who had crossed the bridge at Carjac at the same time as them had bid them farewell before disappearing into the distance in a cloud of chalky dust. Here and there shepherds appeared as tiny black silhouettes amidst their sheep and goats, watching over their flocks in wide open fields bordered by drystone walls and stunted oak trees.

It was hot up on the plateau where there was nothing to shelter them from the sun, and the pilgrims threw back the sides of their mantels so that they flapped behind them like capes. But as they climbed down into a wooded coombe they were struck by the chill in the air. There was a forest of oak trees and sweet chestnuts clinging to the hillside. It was nearly the end of April and the snows were now nothing but a bad memory. Thousands of wild daffodils and hyacinths already brightened the undergrowth with patches of yellow and blue, and filled the air with their heady scent.

The chevalier seemed to notice none of this. He walked beside his brother in silence, his eyebrows knitted, his expression dark. 'Four days since we left Conques,' he was thinking, 'four days and still nothing. The hellish beast is no longer at work. Has it had its fill of blood? Or am I merely a simpleton who has been fooled by it?'

As he walked along pondering, the chevalier watched the sturdy frame of the old *Jacquet* who led his little troop at a good steady pace. Despite his age, he was one of those men who was all nerve and muscle, and who had seemingly boundless energy. And this particular one was as cunning as my lord Fox. But on the night of the murder at the Dômerie Humbert had slept next to Ronan, and the latter had assured him that he could not have got up without waking him, and nor could the mason or his son.

There were the women too . . . But they had slept with Lady Amandine at the Dômerie, and she had not noticed any unexplained absences on that terrible night. Then there were those who had spent the night in the hostel, next to the monks' dorter: Manier, the young shepherd with the blond hair; Arastaigne, the cleric with the vacant, distant expression in his eyes; and the two craftsmen, Master Pierre, the goldsmith from Le Puy, and Master Raoul, the weaver who came from Lyon. There were the three pilgrims, too, who had left the Dômerie after Humbert with the intention of catching up with his group, but who never had . . .

'Galeran!'

'Yes,' said the chevalier with a start. 'What is it, Ronan?'

'Humbert has signalled to us to stop. I think he is having trouble finding his way through all these scrubby little bushes and trees.'

The undergrowth was indeed thick down in the coombe, and it was difficult to see which was the right path. The crosses that had stood all along their route had disappeared, and the old *Jacquet* was hesitating at a fork in the barely visible path which led back up towards the plateau.

'I must have gone wrong somewhere,' he told the chevalier, when he came over. 'If we go that way we'll end up back on the

135

plateau, when we should carry on following the stream down in the coombe. We will have to retrace our steps, my friends.'

Bérengère, who had fallen to the ground when they stopped, was wracked by a bout of coughing. She spoke in breathless snatches, 'Oh, my lord Humbert, I cannot go any further. Could we not stop here a little while longer?'

Humbert turned towards her. The woman's face had turned a chilling shade of grey, her brow gleamed with sweat and, with the dark rings under her eyes, it was painful just to look at her.

He nodded and said, 'We shall make you a litter, Bérengère, and we shall carry you. Try to rest while we are preparing it.'

The poor woman made no protest and curled up on the mossy ground, resting her head on the mantle that her son offered her. The young man watched her anxiously, frequently passing her his calabash to quench the appalling thirst that had gripped her at the same time as her fever.

The weaver took a short axe from his belt and handed it to Ronan who had offered to make the stretcher with Guillaume. Watched by his companions, the troubadour laid into a young hazel tree, felling it with a few powerful blows. He quickly removed the branches from the trunk and cut it into two long poles which they tied together with rope. Then Guillaume threw his mantle over the criss-cross of rope to form a makeshift stretcher.

Once it was ready, they lifted Bérengère onto it carefully. She had sunk into a sleep so deep that even her terrible paroxysms of coughing could not wake her. Her husband and son each took one end of the stretcher, and the little group turned round to retrace its steps.

42

Ronan lengthened his stride and caught up with Bruna. Falling into the same rhythm as her, he said gently, 'May I speak to you, Bruna?'

'If it is to weary me with your oafishness again, keep it to yourself!' replied the girl, without even looking at him.

'Indeed it is not, damsel, what I have to discuss with you is of a most serious nature,' replied the troubadour.

Without slowing her pace, Bruna threw him a sharp sideways glance. Ronan wore an expression she had not seen before.

'You look singularly serious, my Lord de Lesneven!'

'Mock me not and give me an answer, Bruna. By what ill is Lady Freissinge afflicted?'

'And what is it to you, my Lord Most Curious?' retorted Bruna tartly.

'It is, Bruna, that your attitude towards her has changed since we left Conques.'

The young woman's face darkened and she walked on a little faster.

'Whereas before,' insisted Ronan, 'you let her come and go as she pleased, it seems now that you do not take your eyes off her. You even stopped her yesterday in Figeac, when she wanted to walk alone through the town. Why was that?'

'And now he is spying on me on top of everything else!' wailed Bruna, stopping dead and planting her hands on her hips.

Ronan put his hand on her arm.

'No, I want only to help you, Bruna. This woman is a heavy

responsibility for you. She is your mistress, I realise, but all the same . . .'

The young woman shook her arm free and, eyeing the troubadour fiercely, she spat these words at him, 'Stop trying to help me, Ronan de Lesneven! I need no one, least of all you, a rhyme-maker, a . . . a word-juggler!'

Ronan pouted and a mocking smile wiped any gravity from his face.

'Why yes, you are still just as bad-tempered, Untamed damsel, how you deserve your name! But that is precisely why I like you. I would not care for you if you were gentle and tender. I prefer you in your natural state, all nails and teeth bared!'

Flushed with rage, Bruna raised her hand as if she would strike him, then she controlled her emotion, turned on her heel and caught up with Humbert at the head of the group.

43

The old *Jacquet* had found his bearings and now no longer hesitated as he led his little band along a grassy path.

'We shall stop soon,' he told the mason who was walking beside him carrying the stretcher on which his wife lay sleeping. 'It will do us all some good to rest a while, and I remember a good stopping place.'

'Where is that?' asked Garin.

'Very near here, it is called the Antouy chasm.'

The corners of the young man's mouth fell and he said gloomily, 'Well, a chasm hardly sounds a tempting place to rest. It will be as cold and damp as the cave last night.

'Indeed not, you shall see! We shall all sleep outside, and it is a beautiful spot.'

The boy sighed. Since his mother's condition had worsened, he had been quiet and dispirited, unable to take his eyes off her, suffering to see her lying inert as she was jostled between the two shafts of the stretcher.

The *Jacquet* saw him watching her and smiled reassuringly.

'That's another reason we shall stop, Garin. We are going to tend to her; the chevalier, who is familiar with a number of remedies, is going to help me.'

The boy nodded, but said not a word. His eyes were brimming with tears. Humbert patted him affectionately on the shoulder.

'Come on, my son! Take heart. All will be well, you're just tired, we all are! And, my word, you've become a man. Since we left your beard has started sprouting!'

The pilgrims soon came into a clearing, ringed by alders with thick, knotty trunks. Humbert raised his iron staff, indicating that his companions should stop.

'My friends, we shall settle here for the night.'

'But it is still early, it is barely time to eat,' protested the shepherd, pointing to the sun which was still high in the sky.

'That is as may be, Manier. But it will do us the utmost good to take more than a night's rest.'

The shepherd did not insist and turned away, looking for somewhere to put down his few belongings.

'Is this a safe place?' asked the cleric, looking at the surrounding woods suspiciously.

'Yes,' replied Humbert with a laugh. 'Apart from a few wolves that keep themselves to themselves, the place is only used by shepherds and . . . monks. There is a little priory not far from here. I shall go there with Garin to ask for a little bread and milk.'

'I shall come with you,' said the chevalier, handing his bundle of belongings to his brother and following the two men.

'And I shall go and fetch firewood with Arastaigne!' called out the blond shepherd, giving the cleric a hearty slap on the back which made the latter jump with surprise.

The weaver and the goldsmith, their faces tired and drawn, dropped into the tender grass on the ground, only too happy to take off their boots and rub their aching feet. As for Ronan, he watched his brother leaving and then sat down on a tree stump. For the last few nights he had dreamed about walking, and was beginning to wonder if during the daytime he was sleeping when he walked! Humbert was right, a bit of rest would do them all some good.

Noticing Bruna disappearing into the trees, he changed his mind and got up to follow her. Master Pierre, who had seen the Untamed and the troubadour leaving, looked around. Apart from the mason who was tending to his wife, he and the weaver were alone with Lady Freissinge. He put his boots back on quickly and headed for the young woman with an air of determination.

'Let me help you, my lady,' he said, taking the bag that the young woman was rather awkwardly trying to slip off her shoulder. She let him help her without a word. Beneath her hood, which was still lowered despite the heat, the goldsmith could not even make out her eyes. He introduced himself all the same, bowing politely as he had learned to do before his wealthy clients.

'Master Pierre, my lady, for you are a lady, are you not? I can tell from your appearance and from the way you tie your mantle. From your brooch too,' he added, touching the lustrous silver jewel she wore at her throat. The young woman stepped back abruptly, but he went on, unabashed, 'You are most lovely, my lady, I am quite sure of it, and far too young, methinks, to do such harsh penance. Unless, that is, you have done some wrong, committed some sin of the flesh, perhaps?'

He let his words hang in the air, staring at her with his piggy little eyes. Lady Freissinge did not seem to be looking at him, then she suddenly fell to her knees in the grass, her hands clasped across her chest, and lowered her forehead to the ground. The goldsmith hesitated and an expression of disgust swept across his face, then he turned on his heel and went back to the spot he had chosen to sit down.

The weaver, who was sitting on the ground, asked him mockingly, 'Did you want to whisper sweet nothings to her then, Master Pierre?'

'Why not? I'd say the little hussy is most comely,' he replied tartly.

'Comely she may be but with that great cloak and her hood always lowered there is no way of telling, she might be a terrifying vision under all that. I wouldn't want of her, anyway, she has less to say for herself than my spinning wheels! All the time we've been walking I have not heard her complain or breathe a single word!'

'And what of it? Neither has the other one, the Untamed, she does not complain,' retorted Pierre.

'Why yes, but that one bites if you go near her. You only have to see how she brushed Ronan off this morning.'

'For sure. I would not have been happy to be spoken to thus.'

'But with him, it is as if he likes it. He's hot on her heels at this very moment!'

'Forsooth, it is no business of ours when all is said and done. As for the little lady, I have plenty of time, and you shall see, Raoul, we will be more than close friends by the end of the journey.'

The weaver laughed heartily.

'Upon my word! Why exactly are you making this pilgrimage? To pray or perhaps to . . . ?'

The goldsmith eyes him menacingly.

'Fie, fie, my friend,' protested the other. 'I said nothing! Take no offence. It is no business of mine, wouldn't you say? We do what we can with whatever we have! And our reasons for being here are of interest to Saint Jacques and him alone!'

Master Pierre nodded, but said not a word. The weaver shrugged, and went to lie down some way away under a tree.

44

After giving Bérengère a decoction of juniper berries which greatly relieved her suffering, the chevalier had stood watch for much of the night. Eventually he was relieved by Manier and he went and sat against an old tree stump and fell asleep. Not long after, Humbert, who was sleeping not far away, sat up suddenly and held his breath so as to hear the least sound. The chevalier opened his eyes: he too had heard something.

He laid his hand on his companion's arm and whispered, 'Don't move, Humbert, I think it's coming from the chasm.'

From where they were sitting the two men could barely make out the edge of the wood and the clearing around them. The moon was hidden behind a cloud, and the sky was dotted with only a few stars. Everything was reduced to black shadow, from the tops of the trees to the depths of the undergrowth.

The chevalier frowned, wondering what had happened to the shepherd who had taken over from him on watch. He shook his head in irritation when he saw the young man in a deep sleep over by the fire which still exhaled a wisp of white smoke.

It seemed as if the noise was coming from over there. Some tufts of long grass moved, as if swaying in the wind. Then nothing. Whoever or whatever it was, it was moving very slowly.

Humbert had taken up his iron staff without a sound, and Galeran tightened his grip on the hilt of his sword. He screwed up his eyes. The tall grass was parting before a hunched figure. It was at that moment that one of the sleeping figures moaned and rolled over in its sleep, and then everything happened very quickly.

A flash of red light sprang up from the grass and, at the same time, the chevalier and Humbert stood up and shouted at the other pilgrims to flee their assailant. A huge wolf leapt over the shepherd and seized the coney carcass that the men had abandoned by the fire in its great jaws. In a few silent supple strides, the wolf disappeared into a thicket with its meagre booty.

The terrified pilgrims, who had been woken so abruptly by the two men's cries, stood yelling with fear without even knowing why.

'All right, calm down!' exclaimed the chevalier above their wailing. 'There is nothing to fear now, the danger has passed.'

'But what was it?' asked Garin, coming up to the chevalier.

'A wolf, my son, a wolf attracted by the smell of our supper and the remains of the coney we ate last night.'

'Well, that poor grey foot must have been even hungrier than us! There wasn't a scrap left on that carcass.'

Humbert turned to the shepherd who had stood up shakily, speechless with fear, and admonished him roundly, 'You had only two things to do, you worthless wastrel: to bury that carcass as I told you, so as not to attract scavangers, and to take over from the chevalier on watch. You really can be trusted, can you not!'

143

'Forsooth,' added Galeran, eyeing the young man furiously. 'I would be very unwilling to trust my sheep to you, my friend.'

'Oh, very well, very well . . .' grumbled Manier who was now ashamed and embarrassed. 'I was tired, was I not? These things happen!'

'We are all tired, and these things shouldn't happen!' retorted Galeran. The shepherd lowered his head; there was no reply he could give, and he knew it.

'I would like us to have a good look through the woods to see what sort of creature we're dealing with and to see how many of them there are,' said Ronan, going over to his brother with his knife in his hand.

Bruna intervened. 'Nay, you should not all go and get involved,' she said harshly. 'Stay here, all of you, I shall go and see!'

'Are you mad, damsel!' cried the chevalier.

'Why no, my lord, wolves are like my own family, I know how to talk to them!' she said, and disappeared into the thicket with one steady stride, leaving the men to their astonishment. It was Ronan who regained his composure first.

'Do not be afraid for her, I shall follow her,' he said, going into the undergrowth after her. It was pervaded by a peculiar silence, not even disturbed by a breath of wind. The only faint sound was the crystalline tinkling of the river nearby. The moon appeared from behind the clouds and the troubadour soon made out Bruna's outline as she threaded in and out of the trees, climbing over stumps and weaving nimbly between the trunks before coming to a standstill on the edge of the chasm.

What Ronan saw next was beyond belief. The young woman stepped furtively over towards a large wolf which stood motionless as if rooted to the spot. She suddenly fell to the ground onto her back and squirmed at its feet. After a while, the big wolf came and lay down beside Bruna and rolled on its back like her.

144

Eventually, it stood back up and the young woman did the same, standing on all fours. Then Bruna and the wild beast began a game: they took one pace forwards, then stepped back, knocking each other with their heads or their shoulders. To end the game, Bruna simply stood up on her two feet and headed back towards the camp, leaving her playmate behind to stare after her with its yellow eyes. As she passed the thicket in which Ronan was hiding, she tossed him these words, 'You could have ruined everything!' And added, without even turning round, 'It's a she-wolf, she will bear cubs very soon, that's why she likes playing.'

The troubadour was furious, and caught up with her and seized her by the arm.

'You seem to know how to tackle a wolf!'

'Wolves are like dogs, you must simply not be afraid of them.'

'It's a shame I'm not a wolf then!'

She stopped and looked at him searchingly until he felt troubled by her serious stare.

'Yes, my lord, it is a shame,' she said, shaking her arm free from his grasp, 'because wolves are worth far more than some men.'

'What do you mean?'

'Wolves don't kill for pleasure!'

He gave no reply, and they went back to the camp in silence. When they arrived, Bruna told old Humbert, 'There is no danger, my lord, the wolves have other things than us to think about now.'

'By my troth! I'd heard it said,' exclaimed the *Jacquet*, 'but it has to be seen to be believed! So, Bruna, you are a wolf-charmer and you know no fear of them?'

'Oh, I would perhaps not say that, but if you say so, it must be true!' the young woman said calmly and she went back over to her mistress who had stayed by the fire.

After this incident no one could or would go back to sleep. The pilgrims stood around, looking nervously into the shadows which lengthened on the edges of the woods. Seeing that they would not settle again, the chevalier and Humbert revived the fire, and Ronan took up his rebec. He played a few awkward plaintive notes before settling into an old melody from Aquitaine. They all sat down round the flames, forgetting the dark night, caught in the spell of the music.

> 'Oh, Lady Bruna, her son
> was begat by such a moon,
> that he might learn the ways of love.
> Listen, ye all!
> Now, not one did he love
> Nor did any love him . . .'

These were the words Ronan sang, his gaze lost in the distance. Like all the other pilgrims, Bruna could not take her eyes off him, and a strange light shone in her dark eyes. A smile spread across Galeran's face: he recognised this ballad which had been so favoured by his frankly spoken friend, the troubadour Marcabru.*

As the bow hummed over the strings, the stars went out one by one and the sky turned a soft blue. Soon the first ray of sunlight fingered through the tops of the trees. Dawn had arrived: it was time to leave.

Two days later they reached the gates of Cahors. The Antouy chasm and the great wolf they had seen there were already nothing but vague memories.

* See *Blue Blood*.

45

Cahors, which was famous for its powerful bishops and merchants, had known every kind of invading force: the Vikings, the Saracens, the Huns . . . And from all these onslaughts it had emerged above the river Lot proudly bearing its towering fortified walls and the domes of its cathedral. The town rose up from a peninsula like the prow of a ship surrounded by the waters of the wide river. Just one ancient bridge, built by the Romans, gave access to the other bank and facilitated trade with it.

Humbert, who had already stayed in the Cahors region, took his friends straight to the Saint-Jacques sanatorium. It was a wealthy town, and the Lord-Bishop ensured that pilgrims were well looked after there.

A good many pilgrims who had taken shelter in the hospice had left the day before and there was room for all of them. The monks greeted the new arrivals kindly, taking them to a huge vaulted dorter where each was given a rush mat covered with sheepskin. The hall was pleasantly warm thanks to a number of wood burners positioned between the rows of cots.

The father hosteller took their dirty clothes so that they could be cleaned, then, talking to Humbert all the while, he took the pilgrims to the steam room so that they could wash and shave if they chose to. As he left, he told them that while they waited for the evening meal they would be served with a bowl of soup and a glass of wine in the frater.

As for the mason's wife, the monks had taken her stretcher straight to the closed area where the seriously ill were tended.

Only her husband was allowed to go with her. In the last two days Bérengère's condition had deteriorated considerably, despite the attentive care of the chevalier and the old *Jacquet*, and she now had to be carried all the time.

More than once, her husband had been so horrified by her pallor as she lay senseless on the stretcher that he had believed her dead. But each time, Bérengère had regained consciousness, gripping his hand and tearfully begging them not leave her behind.

46

Jaufré, the trusty archer, had told the chevalier that he would take lodgings in the Chapefol Inn near the cathedral of Saint Etienne. The inn was such a narrow building that Galeran would scarcely have noticed it if there had not been a crier outside extolling its virtues that market day.

This particular crier was provoking considerable laughter amongst the passers-by. The inn was named after the game of chapefol or blind man's bluff, and the crier was telling all and sundry that here you could happily, 'Eat and drink with your eyes closed.' The playful passers-by laughed and teased, asking whether they not only had to cover their eyes but also block their ears and noses to enjoy the inn's fare!

Galeran smiled when he heard this jovial repartee, and went into the inn. Apart from the dark figure of the archer, sitting alone at a long table, the room was quite empty. Jaufré was beginning to feel that time was dragging its heels. At first he had strolled aimlessly around the town, but for the last three days he had hardly set foot outside the lower room of the inn watching people as they came in and hoping to see the chevalier's tall figure every time the door opened.

A smile lit up his face when he saw Galeran coming over towards him. The two men greeted each other warmly. Then the chevalier ordered two goblets of barley beer.

'I was beginning to worry about you, my lord,' said Jaufré raising his goblet.

'All is well, my companion. And you? What news?'

'Nothing new here, nor along the way. No victims like the ones we are looking for, my lord. It would seem that our man has been appeased.'

'My news is the same, and I am most disheartened by it.'

'Why so?'

'Since Le Puy, as far as I know, the beast has killed four times. Which leads me to believe two things. Firstly, and this confirms my hypothesis, he must have been alone to begin with and this made it easier for him to strike when and where he wanted. Secondly, and this is more terrible, he could strike very soon, before I have time to flush him out!'

The old archer frowned, wondering how the chevalier reached these conclusions, but Galeran went on, 'This beast is lying in wait, Jaufré, it will not be able to resist the pleasure of killing for long. Its lust for blood is too strong. We can at least be sure of that!'

'Forgive me, my lord, but do you still believe it is with you?'

'I cannot explain why, Jaufré, but I sense it. Besides, it is difficult to say whether my travelling companions deserve to go to heaven or to hell, or to know who they truly are . . . It is even difficult to understand why some of them are making this pilgrimage . . .'

Galeran fell silent. His face was drawn and he seemed tired.

'These long days of walking have changed him,' thought the

old archer. 'Or is it the knowledge that a crime will soon be committed and that he can do nothing to stop it?'

'I spoke to Humbert,' Galeran went on. 'The next major stopping place is Moissac. But between now and then, I have a job for you.'

'Good, my lord, what should I do?'

'Find me someone to take a message to the baron.'

The old archer thought for a moment and then nodded vigorously.

'It shall be done, my lord Galeran, and I cannot even take the credit for it. The provost of Cahors is beholden to the Baron de Peyre. He will find a man for me and will even provide the horse.'

Galeran went on as if talking to himself, 'I shall send a list of the people travelling with me to the baron. Some are meant to be from Le Puy, like the goldsmith, others from the mountains of the Auvergne, like the two women, still others from I know not where. We need him to try and verify these details in the utmost haste.'

'How will he communicate his findings to us?'

'Let us give him a little time. How many days will it take us to reach the mountains from here?'

'I shall have to think on that, my lord,' said the old archer, counting on his fingers. 'Well, at the rate you are progressing, and if you do not stop a while on the way, it should take a good two weeks!'

'That is scarce time for our messenger to go to de Peyre and come back with the findings, but it can be done,' Galeran mused.

'We could ask the Baron de Peyre to send his messenger to Ostabat, either at the meeting of the ways or at the Ospitalia.'

'It shall be thus, and that is where you too shall wait for me,' said the chevalier, taking a sheet of vellum from his pouch to write to the baron. 'When we have eaten, we shall go and see the horses.'

'You miss your charger, do you not?' asked the old archer.

'Indeed yes, Jaufré. He is a long-time companion to whom I owe my life, and I am loathe to travel without him. He is not giving you too much trouble, I trust?'

'No, but his coat has lost its sheen and he will not hold his head high. I think he too is in want of you. He will hold this against you, my lord, and – even if he is carrying little – it is not to his liking to act as a pack horse behind another. It is not in his nature.'

A broad smile lit up the chevalier's face.

'And I understand him well: with his breeding, Quolibet is more inclined to break through enemy ranks on the battlefield! And we too, would you not agree, my friend?'

After eating and drinking copiously, Galeran wrote the letter for the baron. Then at last he went to the nearby stables with Jaufré. As he had predicted, Quolibet was not in good humour, and paid no heed to the chevalier's affectionate greeting. Galeran drew back a little sadly, bid farewell to the old archer and walked briskly back up towards the Saint-Jacques Sanatorium. The oil lamps were being lit along the narrow streets and the heavy cathedral bells were already ringing in the evening Angelus.

47

Garin's legs were quaking with exhaustion, and he had sat down on a barrel to watch the crowd coming and going before the stalls laden with every kind of fish, grain and spice. From this improvised viewpoint on the corner of the rue des Changeurs (the money-changers' street), he was amused by the antics of these serious men, eyeing, weighing, fingering, biting and counting the *florins*, *besants*, *deniers* and every other denomination of coin on their little tables of wood or stone.

There was so much going on in this prosperous town that it made Garin's head spin. And he was tired, so tired. He gave a long yawn and let himself slip to the ground. Just moments later, and despite the jostle and hubbub, he was sleeping like a childer, curled up behind his barrel.

When he woke he thought he recognised a familiar voice: it was coming from the rue aux Tables. Without even getting to his feet, he lifted his head and saw the goldsmith deep in conversation with one of the money-changers.

Master Pierre had put a piece of metal on the table. First the money-changer weighed it up in his hand, then he put it onto the scales. Without coming out of hiding Garin could not hear everything the two men were saying, but he very soon understood that they did not agree on the value of the metal. The boy had never seen money like that in his life, and could not know that this strange little piece of metal was in fact a *marka* of pure silver.

Master Pierre raised his voice, pointing to the white metal, 'I am a goldsmith myself,' he said. 'I know what things are worth as well as you do.'

The money-changer raised his voice in turn, 'You may well know the prices, but I am telling you that it has been trimmed, my lord goldsmith, and that is crime enough to send you to the stocks!'

'Forsooth, you are all thieves here in Cahors!' cried Master Pierre, glowering at the other man. Then he snatched the coin angrily from him, put it back in his pouch and left abruptly, not even noticing Garin as he passed him.

The young man stood up and stretched for some time. A little way away on the big square he saw the solitary figure of Arastaigne slipping into a narrow passageway.

Garin set off across town, choosing his route at random, and soon came to the ramparts rising dramatically above the waters of the Lot which were swollen with meltwater. He stayed there for some time, leaning against the parapet, watching pieces of wood tossed by the raging currents. He was still there when the evening Angelus rang, and he decided to hurry back to the hospice.

48

At nightfall this area was a gloomy place, little more than a vast field of ruins, bordered on one side by the cob-built cottages of the poorer quarters and on the other by an impenetrable thicket of brambles. Ancient oak trees had insinuated their roots between the crumbling remnants of the walls, and the pallid remains of marble statues were cloaked in ivy. Stone columns, sculpted capitals and fractured pediments lay randomly on the ground like an immense labyrinth of rubble which no longer led anywhere.

Garin looked round anxiously. He really was lost in this accursed town, and these must be the ruins of the Roman quarter, a reminder of a pagan past that the inhabitants of Cahors preferred not to frequent – especially at night. The young man was not very bold by nature but he slipped his hands into his belt, whistled a little ditty and set off at a good pace.

At first he walked as best he could along open ground, but suddenly he found himself in front of a huge building which had remained almost intact. Humbert had told him that the old thermal baths still stood, as did the old theatre, the Cirque des Cadourques, where great massacres had been carried out in the past. Garin went under a wide porch and climbed a few steps which led to a dark corridor. A feeble rectangle of light seemed to indicate the other end of the narrow tunnel. The boy suddenly felt as if he were caught in a trap, and he ran frantically towards the light, arriving, with his heart pounding in his chest, at an open platform under the great evening sky. He bent over, with his hands on his knees, and tried to pull himself together and to breathe more slowly.

When at last he stood up again he looked round at the tiers and tiers of stone steps that rose up above him. He was in the middle of the ancient amphitheatre, a single building which was bigger than the whole village in which he had been born.

It was growing dark. The first stars were appearing in the sky and the shadows were lengthening, sidling along the stones covered in grey lichen. That was when he heard footsteps. Footsteps that were coming ever closer and reverberating throughout the amphitheatre. Garin looked round but, because of the echo, it was impossible to tell where they were coming from.

The footsteps had stopped.

'Garin!' called a voice, and a series of echoes picked it up. 'Garin! Garin, where are you?'

The sound was distorted and amplified as it was relayed endlessly from one tier to another.

'I'm here!' cried the young man. 'But who are you? Where are you? I can't find my way in here . . .'

There was a peal of laughter very close to him and then silence. Startled, he tripped and fell, sprawling in the rubble, knocking against something hairy and sticky. At first he thought it was the carcass of a large animal that someone had dumped there. Then he realised to his horror that what he had grabbed was a fur mantle and that underneath it was a human form, a stiffened body, which he tried in vain to turn over. The man was certainly dead, more than dead.

Garin stood up and swore loudly as if to drive away the revulsion and fear that possessed him. He stumbled away in the half light. Before him he could see the vague outline of the doorway into the arena and a porch that had partly crumbled away. As he neared it a hand grabbed his hood and pulled him backwards.

He screamed and spun round raising his knee where he estimated it would do the most damage to his assailant. The other let go of him with a wail of pain and rolled onto the ground.

'But, are you mad? Do you want to kill me?'

The voice was familiar, but Garin still could not identify it. He had taken out his knife and stood just a few paces away from the stranger, his face flushed, his legs braced for action. The other was still groaning and rolled onto one side to stand up.

'Whoever you are,' growled Garin, 'don't move or I shall use my knife!'

It was so dark that the young man could not make out the other man's features.

'But, in the name of heaven, do you not recognise me? It is I, Manier! Manier, the shepherd. Why did you strike me?' he asked with his hands on his groin. 'I called you. I saw you in the streets a while ago and then you disappeared. I thought you'd lost your way so I came to look for you.'

Garin hesitated. Since the incident in the barn, he had been wary of the shepherd, but it certainly was his voice. A little shame-faced, he asked, 'Why was that then, why did you come looking for me?'

'Well, I know my way round here. I've already been here with the mule drivers from Galicia and I know how easy it is to get lost in these ruins.'

Garin did not reply straight away. He kept thinking about the man lying dead not far away and an edge of fear came into his voice as he asked, 'Have you seen the body then?'

'What?' asked the other in amazement. 'Which body?'

'There's a man there, just there, he's dead,' whispered the young man.

'You'll bring us bad luck with your tales! Are you mad? You're like your mother, you must be feverish!'

'Don't bring my mother into this!' growled Garin, and Manier raised his hands as if to protect himself.

'Fie, fie! I meant no harm in saying that. But no, I have not seen a body. Where is this body of yours?'

'There, just there, I said!'

They suddenly fell silent, as they heard a loud clashing of weapons. Before they had time to react, the arena was lit by several torches and they were surrounded by a company of the provost's men.

An unusually tall man called to them, 'So, my little lambs, it's springtime and we felt like going for a nice little walk, did we? And what's that knife for, then?' he added wrenching Garin's knife from his hand.

'It's to defend myself,' protested the young man.

'To defend youself from what?'

'Well, from him, at least that's what I thought. He was following me in the ruins and I did not recognise him, so I took out my knife. I was trying to get back to the Hospice of Saint-Jacques, we're travelling to Compostela.'

'We are *Jacquets*,' added Manier who had stood up with a grimace of pain.

The sergeant raised his torch and peered at the two faces before him.

'Sergeant! Sergeant!' cried one of the armed men who had moved off into the ruins. 'Come over here.'

The old officer's face darkened. He said crisply, 'You two, follow me! I'm not sure that we've finished with you yet!'

'Yes, Sergeant, that's just what I wanted to tell you,' said Garin, coming closer to him.

'To tell me what?'

'That I tripped over a dead body,' replied the young man, not realising that such an avowal could see him condemned. The sergeant nodded and turned away without a word.

One of the armed men stood with his torch raised at the spot where Garin had fallen to the ground. The flickering light revealed the motionless body covered by its mantle. The sergeant leant over it and lifted the hood which hid the dead man's face. He touched the ice-cold features.

'Well, what a pretty piece of work. Come over here, you,' he said, turning to Garin, 'and look at this.'

The young man did as he was told and recoiled in horror, his face as white as linen.

'God help us. How gruesome! Oh, God help us!'

The sergeant watched him impassively, while Manier cried out, 'What did you see, Garin, what did you see? What is it?'

157

Garin gave no reply, he was sickened by what he had seen. The whole episode seemed like a bad dream.

'You, keep quiet,' the sergeant ordered the shepherd. 'You two, take this whippersnapper to the provost for me. We'll join you there later.'

Two of the men grabbed Manier, and soon Garin could only hear their footsteps fading in the distance, then silence fell around him again. He was alone with the sergeant and the rest of the patrol. The old soldier suddenly thumped him on the back.

'Come on, my boy, wake up! Haven't you ever seen a man with his throat cut?'

Garin shook his head.

'Not very pretty, is it? Even so, whoever did this had a very steady hand. You can take it from me and my years of experience that it's not easy cutting someone's throat with one clean stroke, you have to know what you're doing, you have to be in the habit of it, some would say!'

'What do you want from me?' hissed the young man. 'What are we staying here for?'

'We're very happy here. I don't like rushing things,' replied the old man, driving his torch into the ground and sitting down on a block of stone as if it were a throne. 'And the rest of you, you lazy lot, keep looking! You and you, look after the body and check over this boy first.'

Without a word the men set to work. The old soldier obviously knew how to make people obey him. Having searched Garin from head to foot, one of the men leant over the body while the other held his torch up to light it. He turned it over, took off its boots and the fine mantle, feeling every last fold in the clothes. And all the while the other men from the patrol walked methodically through the ruins holding their torches aloft.

158

'Now sit down, my boy. And tell me what you know.'

'But, but . . .' stammered Garin, impressed by the old soldier's calm.

'You know this man, don't you?'

'Yes,' breathed the young man. 'He's one of the men travelling in the group with us.'

'Who do you mean by "us"?'

'My father and my mother and Humbert and, well, everyone who's waiting for me at the hospice.'

'I see, at the Saint-Jacques Sanatorium, you mean? That's what you said earlier.'

'Yes, that's right.'

'Who is this man?'

'He's a goldsmith. From Le Puy, I think. His name is Master Pierre. That's all I know.'

'Indeed it is not, my boy, you must know a lot more. Tell me a bit about your travelling companions.'

Garin did as he was told, gradually relaxing as he answered the sergeant's questions. The flame from the torch which had been planted into the ground threw distorted shadows on the ancient walls, and Garin talked – and talked.

The man who had searched the body came back over to them and announced, 'Nothing, Sergeant.'

'By my troth, what do you mean nothing?' said the old man-at-arms.

'No jewels, no baggage, no purse nor no weapons neither, but his boots wasn't taken nor his mantle and them's worth their weight in gold.'

Garin hesitated. He now remembered the rue aux Tables and the strange coin on the money-changer's scales. The sergeant sensed that something was troubling him.

'What is it, my boy? Speak . . .' he coaxed him.

'He had money, the goldsmith did. This very afternoon he was

159

in the money-changers' street. I saw him.' And Garin related to them the conversation he had overheard.

'A piece of white metal, you say? How big was it?'

'Like this,' said Garin, forming the shape with his fingers.

The sergeant whistled.

'This fellow was wandering about with a silver *marka* in his pockets, or several perhaps! Even if it had been trimmed, this *marka* of his, men have been killed for less than that. Would you recognise the money-changer?'

'Probably,' replied Garin, and then after a brief silence he added, 'Tell me, Sergeant, do you think I am guilty of all this?'

'What do you think, my boy?'

Garin thought for a moment and then announced, 'It seems to me that you could. I had a knife in my hand when you found me, I know the dead man and I even knew that he had money on him, a lot of money if I've understood you right.'

'Why, yes,' said the sergeant gruffly. 'You could indeed end up in gaol or, worse, on the gallows.' Garin paled at these words. 'But,' went on the other, 'it's because of all this that you will, in fact, be set free. If the provost will hear my reasoning.'

Garin gave no reply, his heart was pounding and he thanked God that he had fallen into the hands of a wily fox who was not as heartless as his gruff manner implied.

'Sergeant, look what I've found!' cried one of the men, holding up a slender knife with a bloodied blade.

'Well done, you worthless bunch. All right then, let's go home. A good fire, a good meal, a good bed, that's what we need now.'

'Is that what he was killed with?' breathed the young man.

'Well, it certainly looks like it, my boy! And this blade is far better adapted to the particular job it had to perform than your one, and it's a good sight sharper as well,' he said, running his finger over the blade.

'And Manier, do you believe he is guilty?' asked Garin on the way back.

'I know not, my boy. I shall take my time in questioning him. Is he a friend of yours?'

'Why no,' replied Garin rather more sharply than he would have wanted.

'So much the better, because he looks every inch a rascal to me, and I wouldn't be prepared to swear to his morals or his righteousness,' grumbled the sergeant. 'You see, boy, when we reached this unfortunate body it was already cold and covered in dew. If you had killed him, you and the shepherd would have fled much earlier.'

'So you believe me. You will let us go?' cried Garin.

The old soldier appeared not to have heard the question. They arrived in front of the postern of the gaol with its iron bars. The guards stood aside and the heavy door closed slowly behind them.

49

The sergeant most certainly did take his time.

Garin and Manier spent the rest of the night at the gaol in the company of a vicious family of rats in a cell that reeked of urine.

The following morning the sergeant went to the Saint-Jacques hospice where he interviewed the monks and the *Jacquets* individually and had his men search through their meagre belongings. Galeran and Humbert were summoned to identify the body of the goldsmith, and the men-at-arms took them to the lower room where he had been laid out.

In the money-changers' quarter Garin found the trader who

had accused the goldsmith of trimming his coin. He too formally identified the body of the victim: that was indeed the man, he announced, who had been walking through the streets of Cahors with a whittled-down *marka*.

The provost, who had set off for the Marches, had entrusted the whole business to the sergeant who released Garin that same evening. As for Manier, he spent two more days at the gaol but, as there was no evidence against him, he too was released.

In any event, according to the sergeant who stuck resolutely to his own deductions, the wound which had taken the goldsmith's life was the work of a hardened killer and not some shepherd or young mason. He was more suspicious of a gang of thugs who were terrorising the townspeople of Cahors at the time. They had lost count of the thefts, attacks and break-ins committed by these crooks who were giving the provost and his men plenty to worry about.

'These thugs are capable of anything,' the sergeant explained to the chevalier and Humbert. 'They needed only to see what the goldsmith was up to with his *marka*, and, well, it was only a matter of time before they committed murder!'

The following morning the case was closed. Master Pierre's body was buried and the pilgrims left Cahors for Gascony.

PART FIVE

And the Lord set a mark upon Cain
lest any finding him should kill him.

Genesis 4:15

50

Since the goldsmith's death something within the little group had been lost for ever. It was not that Master Pierre had been particularly liked, but he had been one of their number, and his mysterious end left the band of travellers feeling vulnerable and afraid.

After leaving Cahors, when they next stopped to rest beside a stream, the chevalier took Humbert to one side.

'I have scarce had the time to speak to you since our last conversation, my lord Humbert,' said Galeran, leaning up against a tree. The *Jacquet* sat down on a tree stump, laid down his travelling bags and looked up at him.

'It is true, Chevalier. But I knew that you would come to me eventually.'

'The other day you wished to know why I was making this journey with you. I shall tell you why, Humbert, and I shall ask you to treat this knowledge as a secret.'

The old man shrugged but said not a word.

'I perform a most unpleasant kind of work,' Galeran spat out, eyeing the old man's face. But his excess of emotion was wasted, the old traveller did not turn a hair. He sat with his arms crossed over his chest, apparently prepared for whatever the chevalier might have to say to him. So Galeran proceeded to tell him what he knew about this murderous beast, sparing him none of the details, even the most repulsive. The only thing he kept to himself, and it was some omission, was Jaufré's involvement and the link with the Baron de Peyre.

When he had finished, the old man looked up at him strangely, with a mixture of weariness and determination in his expression.

'You know, Chevalier, in all these years I believe I have travelled alongside some fairly dubious characters. Wastrels, thieves, probably even murderers, but I have never wanted to think about what they really were . . .' he let his words hang in the air.

'And this time, Humbert?'

As if he did not wish to reply, the old man threw Galeran a question of his own. 'But the goldsmith's death, Chevalier, why did you not tell me anything?'

'It is true, Humbert. I am perplexed by this death. The slit throat and the trimmed *marka* are hardly in keeping with the killer I am looking for, and yet . . .'

'And yet?'

'And yet there is a link, I would stake my honour on it!'

'What link?' asked the old man.

'The link is our group, Humbert!'

The old pilgrim sat speechless. He stared at the chevalier, his face tense and his jaw clamped in silence.

'Our group which – according to all your accounts, which I have checked – was joined by my brother and the two townsmen after Aumont. Our group which was later joined by Arastaigne and Manier the shepherd, while you were still in the lands of the Baron de Peyre. Our group, above all, which left the Dômerie leaving behind it the corpse of a young novice, butchered like all those that had been found before! Our group, finally, which has just lost one of its number in a violent death. And that, my lord Humbert, is a new departure.'

'And what if you were wrong, Galeran?'

'I should be happy if that were the case, Humbert,' replied the chevalier wearily. 'I would like this all to be a bad dream and for the white path not to be sullied by blood!'

The old man seemed to reach a decision.

'What is it that you would like me to do, Chevalier? You do not strike me as a man who was merely looking for someone to confide in.'

'My lord Humbert, I would like your opinion. Just your opinion on each of the men with whom you have been travelling for a good deal longer than I, and some of whom may just have opened their hearts to you.'

'I believe in redemption, Galeran. I believe that many of these men and women are going to Compostela in search of redemption, and I put little store by what they are or what they might have done. As for those who may have confided in me, I shall not betray them,' said the *Jacquet*.

'I seek nothing other than this killer of young men,' protested Galeran.

'Perhaps, Chevalier, you cannot imagine what it is you might discover!' said the old man, leaning on his stick to stand up.

'What do you mean, Humbert?'

'Nothing more than I said, Chevalier. I shall keep your secret as I have the secrets of the others, and I shall take you to Compostela as I shall them, if you so wish, nothing more.' With these words, Humbert walked slowly away, and Galeran made no attempt to stop him.

The chevalier dropped to the ground at the foot of the tree. A stony anger rose up within him, anger against himself, against his brother, against Humbert, against every obstacle that stood in his way, masking the truth from him. A truth that he sometimes felt he could almost touch before it slipped away.

He thought carefully about each of his travelling companions. Master Raoul who, since the goldsmith's death, had divided his time between prayer and bouts of heavy drinking with Ronan. Manier, the young shepherd, who hardly ever left Arastaigne's side. Garin who had descended into silence since the goldsmith's death and his own brief imprisonment. And Guillaume the mason, who seemed to be wasting away gradually like his wife. His hair had turned white in just one night, putting years beyond his natural age on him. The prediction that Humbert had made before their departure was coming true. The pilgrimage was doing its work and transforming them, revealing to them what they least wanted to see, what they were afraid to see.

Galeran looked up. Raoul was calling him. The old *Jacquet* had given the signal to leave, and the pilgrims were getting to their feet. He took up his bag and went back to them, standing close to Bérengère's stretcher. Garin was talking to his father, his voice thick with emotion.

'We shall have to stop in a hospice. Mother was so much better when we were in Cahors. She needs warmth and proper care. It's this journey which is taking her from us.'

The mason shook his head stubbornly without even giving a reply.

'I cannot stop, Garin, I do not wish to,' whispered Bérengère. 'I want to go to Saint-Jacques. I must, do you see!'

Even though he knew he would obey her wishes, the young man protested. He kept looking at her thin drawn face, amazed that it could still be fired by such a strong will.

'But you need to get better first, and you will never get better like this, even if father and I carry you all the way there.'

The woman's face looked even more gaunt and drawn as she clutched her son's hand in her bony fingers, 'I'm going to die, Garin, I know that. Don't leave me. I want to go further, always further, to the far side of the hills. Swear to it, my son, swear that you will take me . . .'

And Garin swore, although his eyes were blinded by tears that would not flow.

The chevalier, who had heard everything, leant towards the young man and said firmly, 'Here, Garin, give me the stretcher, I will carry it for a while. You can take over again in a moment.'

The young man hesitated before agreeing with a nod of his head, and Galeran took up the shafts of the stretcher. Despite his exhaustion, Garin strode out quickly and his stiff, adolescent frame soon reached the head of the group and drew ahead of it swiftly.

51

Three days later, having toiled through the dry white hills of Quercy, the travellers found themselves in wooded valleys and then on the plain of the river Tarn dominated by the abbey at Moissac.

These former marshes – where Clovis was meant to have stood before a thousand monks and thrown his javelin to mark the foundation of his abbey – had been drained, and now there were fertile fields stretching before them to the foot of the town's ramparts.

It was Sunday, and the bells were jubilantly ringing in High Mass. A dense crowd thronged at the town gates. Carts laden with whole families of peasants mingled with the pilgrims and the traders. Everyone was heading up towards the abbey where Abbot Géraud stood waiting to welcome the faithful.

After celebrating Mass, the pilgrims had dispersed around Moissac. Ronan had headed off with Raoul and Manier to have a drink in an inn not far from the abbey. Humbert and Arastaigne were in conversation with a group of pilgrims who had come from Le Puy like themselves. Galeran found himself with the Untamed and her mistress. He held out his hand to the young woman and said, 'I saw a fountain over there. Give me your aquamaniles, damsels, and I shall fill them for you.'

Bruna, always defiant, hesitated, and Galeran smiled at her.

'Why so wary, damsel? I promise I shall not run off with them.'

'You mock me, Chevalier.'

'It is true,' he said, 'and I beg your pardon for it most earnestly, but since we have been travelling, you have made such obvious efforts to avoid me.'

'It is not that I am avoiding you, my lord,' retorted the girl.

'Where is it that you come from then, damsel Bruna, that you are so stubborn? Where I come from, in Brittany, girls are said to have heads as hard as granite, so stubborn are they!'

The young girl smiled weakly. She had dark rings under her eyes, and wisps of hair escaped from her dishevelled plaits. She looked spent, exhausted.

The chevalier said gently, 'I have a proposal for you, damsel Bruna. First of all we shall go and eat, with your mistress. I am inviting you both, and afterwards, if you would still like to, I shall tell you about my home, and you can tell me about yours.'

Still wearing her stubborn expression, the girl announced, 'I have no wish to go and eat in an inn with my mistress.'

'Let it be as you wish. We shall eat out on the grass,' replied the chevalier. 'I saw a girl over there selling pâté, dumplings and eggs. I shall buy some for you, and a little wine.' And before Bruna could refuse, the chevalier had left.

She watched him moving off into the crowd and sighed. She felt so tired. Before making this pilgrimage she had never even imagined that you could feel so tired in body and soul.

'Come, damsel,' said a clear, friendly voice in her ear.

She was startled, because she had not seen the young chevalier coming back. His hands were laden with victuals, and he was carrying a calabash full of wine.

'There's a meadow with some shady trees behind the abbey, two minutes from here, are you coming?'

Bruna suddenly realised how hungry she was. No longer hesitating, she took Lady Freissinge's hand, tossed her bag over her shoulder and followed the chevalier who had already set off.

Galeran waited for them under a blossoming cherry tree which hummed with bees. When he saw them both coming over he wondered which was the other's shadow. He threw his mantle down on the tender young grass and gestured to the two women to sit down, before sitting down opposite them himself.

'Now I have a mind to finish off all these fine things!' he said, cutting two thick slices of pâté and putting them on some leavened bread. Bruna's eyes shone as she took her share and she devoured it eagerly, while her mistress broke hers into smaller pieces which she nibbled daintily, raising her hood just enough to put the morsels between her lips.

Galeran smiled, passed them the calabash full of diluted wine, and then handed them two large dumplings filled with honey. Bruna sighed with satisfaction and, brushing aside an opportunist wasp, licked her fingers contentedly. Some of the colour had come back to her cheeks and she burst out laughing quite spontaneously.

'My God, I was so hungry. Thank you, Chevalier, that is the best meal I have had for a long time.'

'My thanks to you, damsel. You look much better for it, you know.'

'Why do you take an interest in me, my lord?' the young girl asked suddenly, wiping her mouth with a corner of her shift.

Now it was Galeran's turn to laugh.

'Why it is only normal, damsel. Do you not take an interest in your fellow creatures, even if they walk on all fours and have russet hair?'

The young woman raised her hand in an access of temper, but let it fall back onto her knee.

'You are crafty, my lord, like your brother whose tongue is far too sharp . . . and yet you are scarce alike.'

'I know not whether that is a compliment coming from you, damsel,' replied the chevalier. 'But, tell me, what do you think of Ronan?'

Bruna thought for a moment and then announced with aplomb.

'I have watched you, the two of you. And I have thought that you and your brother are far from devoted to each other. You no longer even walk together. When he goes off to drink and make merry, it is with Raoul or Manier, rarely with you.'

A thin smile settled on the chevalier's face.

'It is true, damsel, that I was very young when Ronan left our home to see the world, and life has kept us apart. When I met him in Conques, it was nearly ten years since I had seen him.'

'But why, if you do not have much affection for each other, are you making this pilgrimage with him?' asked the discerning Bruna.

The chevalier hesitated and then gave the simple reply, 'After all these years, I did not know what sort of man my brother had become, damsel. I was hoping that the white path would bring us together and, by my faith, I hope so still.'

The girl flushed, a little embarrassed, and nodded her head.

'Forgive me, my lord, I did not mean to . . .'

'There is no harm in what you ask, damsel,' said the chevalier lightly. 'But it is your turn now. Tell me about yourself!'

'What do you wish to know?' she said, picking a pink clover flower and sucking its petals as if they were sweetmeats.

172

'Ronan told me that you are from the Auvergne mountains. Is that so?'

'I was born there, indeed yes, my lord, as was my mother and my mother's mother before her. And, until very recently, I lived in the mesne on the estates of Lord d'Apchon.'

'It is a wild place, and a harsh place to live from what I have heard?'

The young girl's answer was given with defiant energy which made the chevalier smile. 'It is my home, Chevalier!' And she went on speaking as if she could suddenly see the scenery of her childhood unfolding before her eyes, 'I am from Nérestang, in the Falgoux valley. It is a hamlet, with a fortified house hard up against the cliffs of the Angouran rocks. That is where I came into the world, in that coombe where the waters of the Loudeyre stream run clear.'

'Nérestang – what a pretty name,' murmured the chevalier. 'It probably comes from the Latin *nigrum stagnum* . . .'

'What are you saying, Chevalier? Do you understand Latin like a cleric?'

'I was saying that the name of your village means "the black that remains", "the darkness that stays" or something like that.'

Amazed, Bruna murmured, 'Yes, you are right, Chevalier, it must be so. Even though I do not understand the language of the church, the valley is closed in and there is always shadow on one of the slopes when the others are in sunlight. "The darkness that stays", just as you said!'

They remained silent for a long time, lost in their thoughts, and the only sound was the gurgling of a nearby stream. Eventually, Galeran rose to his feet and indicated that Bruna should follow him. When they were some distance from Lady Freissinge, the chevalier asked quietly, 'Why did you agree to make this pilgrimage, Bruna, particularly with a woman you must watch so closely?'

'I am a free woman, but I gave my word, my lord! Therefore, my master will take care of my mother who is a widow and has only me, should I not return to my homeland.'

'But why has Lord d'Apchon set his wife on this terrible journey, because she is his wife, is she not? With no escort but an inexperienced young girl, rather than two armed men?'

The young woman's face darkened. She turned away, waving to her companion to join them.

'It is not my business, my lord, I am given orders and I obey. I have done so all my life and will never turn against it. Now, we must go and find our companions. Thank you again for such an excellent meal.'

The chevalier nodded.

'It is true that the explanation for all this is no business of mine, Bruna. But perhaps I may know a remedy for your mistress's suffering?'

The young woman was standing stock still and her lips trembled as if she were about to speak, but she overcame the impulse.

'I think not, Chevalier, and there is no need to agonise over it. We are already far along on our journey, and it will surely cure my mistress of her ills. And the fact that two women are making the pilgrimage alone need not be seen as a great mystery.'

The chevalier put up his hand as if to protest, but Bruna stood firm like a defiant little cockerel and went on, 'And, even if I am not an armed man, as you say, perhaps I am not an inexperienced young girl, either.'

With these words, the Untamed put her arm around her companion's waist and led her away with a playful laugh.

52

To leave Moissac, the pilgrims had to take a towpath along the banks of the Tarn until they reached La Pointe where an old ferry would take them to the opposite bank. It was here that the river joined the Garonne. But that year the meltwater had made the waters swell more than usual. The outskirts of the town were flooded, and, despite their best efforts, the pilgrims came to a stop, shin-deep in water, in front of the church of Saint Martin.

Below them, boats glided swiftly between the willows and elms along what had been the towpath. The monks had warned Humbert that the lower parts of the town were flooded, but the old *Jacquet* had not thought it would be this bad. Seeing the torrenting water slapping against the side of the cliffs he understood why so many pilgrims had taken refuge with the locals before setting off again.

He hailed an old man who was coming out of his house with his breeches pulled up above his knees.

'God be with you, my good man, we are pilgrims and we need to get to the ferry at La Pointe.'

'By my troth, it ain't possible, sire!' cried the old man. 'You'll not get so far as the ferry. We's already up to our ankles in it here, and we's afeared of being carried away. Y'll be needing a boat to get there, but – even then – I wouldn't be a-risking of it. It's so bad that the hospital at La Pointe has been evacuating of the sick up onto higher ground.'

'Is the ferry still operating?'

'Why yes, but since the water's been rising, it's been a-going over to La Bernade, but that's because of the cattle market and all.'

Humbert thought for a moment and then said decisively, 'We cannot stay here. Which way can we go to get to La Pointe?'

'It'll be difficult, you know, specially with a stretcher,' said the old man, nodding towards Bérengère.

'You must surely know a route that would get us there,' coaxed Humbert.

'Hmm. Head that way,' said the old man, holding his stick up towards a track which led up the hillside. 'If you can get through on that track, follow it all the way to the Madeleine farm in the dell. When you be a-reaching the round rock, take the grassy pathway and that'll be taking you all the way to the hospital at La Pointe.'

'And is the ferryman willing to take pilgrims?'

'If you has an extra little prayer for him and a spare coin or two,' said the other, with a wink of his eye, 'he'll see what he can do for *Jacquets* like yourselves. He's a cousin of mine, tell him old Joseph sent you. We all has to help each other in this life, doesn't we?'

53

The ferry at La Pointe was a large log raft which was hauled along sturdy ropes, making it glide slowly over the river. On the opposite bank an elderly shepherd with his goats was waiting for it in the shade of an elm tree. The pilgrims stood on the raft heaving on the ropes which hung above the dirty water. The raft was heavily laden and it was difficult to manoeuvre, because the ferryman had insisted on taking several head of cattle as well.

They had left the bank, a huge quagmire oozing with black water, and had only just edged beyond La Pointe. The waters still carried all sorts of dangerous flotsam – tree trunks and even the monstrously swollen carcasses of animals – which had to be kept away from the raft with long poles.

The ferryman, who watched every flicker of the current with an anxious eye, suddenly yelled, 'Look out! Straight ahead. Hang on to the rope! It's coming straight for us!'

The pilgrims grabbed hold of the rope, and the ferry shuddered to a halt, but they could not avoid a huge tree which was bearing down on them with its branches raised out of the water. It struck them with a dull thud, knocking the ferry off course. The rope stretched almost to breaking point as they held fast to it, and people screamed and cried at the other end of the raft. Garin, who had rushed to his mother's side where she lay on her stretcher, tripped and fell overboard.

Before anyone had time to intervene, they saw the Untamed dive into the filthy seething water and try to catch hold of the young man who seemed to have lost consciousness.

'Don't let go of the rope!' yelled the ferryman taking his axe to the branches which had become entangled in it. With a few vigorous blows he brought the boughs crashing down onto the front of the ferry, and the massive trunk was swept away from it by the current.

'Help me!' cried Bruna who, by some miracle, had reached Garin and was holding his head out of the water, but could not heave him on board. The chevalier rushed over, grabbed the young man by the hair and then got hold of him under his arms. He heaved him onto the raft with Ronan's help.

Bruna herself managed to get back on board without help from anyone, as with everything else. She was covered in foul black mud and shivering with the cold. She wrapped herself gratefully in the blanket offered to her by the troubadour who sang, 'She was black but beautiful, the queen whom Solomon loved!'

For once she did not reply. She could not take her eyes off Garin who lay lifeless at the chevalier's feet. The young man seemed to have stopped breathing, and Galeran knelt beside him. He quickly wiped away the filth that was obstructing his mouth, and pulled his head backwards. Then he leant forward, pinched the boy's nostrils and, pressing his lips onto his, blew air into his lungs once, and then twice.

Everyone stood gripping the rope with whitened knuckles, the *Jacquets* and the ferryman alike watching the chevalier's efforts in tense silence. Garin's ribcage suddenly heaved and he coughed up some of the filthy water. He was saved! Galeran helped him sit up, and Bruna came over to sit beside him.

The chevalier stood up and gestured to Humbert and Guillaume that all was well. Bérengère lay unconscious, unaware of what had happened, which was probably just as well for her peace of mind.

'What happened?' Garin sobbed, rubbing his throat. 'I feel as if I drank the whole river.'

'That is not far from the truth,' said Ronan with a laugh. 'Luckily for you, the Untamed stopped you draining the whole flagon!'

The young man turned to Bruna and saw the piteous state she was in.

'Was it you who saved me?' he whispered softly.

The Untamed stood up as if she had been bitten. When she did reply, her voice was harsh, 'Well, don't look at me with those great big eyes. Anyway, I was the closest. And if it had not been for the chevalier you would have been a dead man.' And, still wearing her stubborn expression, she took up her place again along the rope, deliberately turning her back on him.

The ferry bumped into the far bank and the ferryman secured

the rope, setting the gangplank down onto a mound of earth which had been built up out of the mud. After thanking him, the pilgrims stepped onto the flooded bank, carrying their belongings on their heads. Humbert took up the lead, and Ronan and Galeran took up Bérengère's stretcher decisively and put the poles onto their shoulders.

The meadow looked like a black sheet which heaved and plunged with each of their footsteps. They made slow progress, with water right up to their thighs at times, and they clung to each other so as not to be carried away by the current, heading for the elm where the old shepherd had been waiting with his goats. At least there they would be dry.

From time to time, ducks or moorhens would take to the air, alarmed by their cumbersome passage. At last they reached dry ground and, with filthy clothes and boots filled with cloying mud, they dropped exhausted onto the grass. A warm wind stroked their faces. Humbert sat up, wetted his index finger and held it up to establish the direction of the wind.

'That is a southerly, is it not?' asked Ronan who had watched this simple trick.

'It is indeed,' replied Humbert. 'There is rain to come. Why, that is just what we needed!' he added wryly.

54

When the rain came it was heavy, even torrential, as it can be in the south. It whipped their faces, soaked their clothes and drowned their shoes. It tore branches from the trees and transformed the muddy paths into rivulets of yellowish sludge in which the travellers slipped and tripped. Three days of walking through the Gascony hills brought the little band to the gates of the town of Lectoure in a piteous state.

Then, just as quickly as it had started, the deluge stopped, giving way to a devastatingly blue sky. The former Gallo-Roman town, with the standard of the Viscountcy de Lomagne fluttering on its ramparts, proudly looked down on the surrounding peaks from its rocky vantage point. It was market day in the upper part of town, and the pilgrims decided to buy some provisions because what little food they had left had been ruined in their musty, wet travelling bags.

With their mantles soaked and splattered with mud, they looked so pitiful that they could have been mistaken for a band of thieves, were it not for Humbert's impressive cape with its three shells and his proud expression. They bought a little fresh bread, salted meat and cheese, and the *Jacquet* led them through the sloping little streets to the Houndélia fountain. There they sat down and began to eat.

'It is said,' began the old *Jacquet*, indicating the pool of limpid water, 'that this source used to be dedicated to the goddess Diana. To this day the people of Lectoure throw coins into it to win the favour of this powerful divinity.'

'All right, all right,' grumbled the cleric, filling his calabash. 'That is all very nice, this may well be dedicated to some goddess or other, but I say we've had our fill of water. Pray, when are we going to stop, Humbert? We cannot go on, and look at the state we are in, not one dry hair on our bodies, our faces so haggard we frighten children in the street.'

'Why should we not stop here?' added the shepherd with a note of bitterness in his voice.

'There is no room left either in the hospice or in private homes,' said Humbert, looking round at the mud-splattered faces that had turned to him for a solution.

'What about in the lower part of town?'

'It is the same throughout Lectoure. Our fellow *Jacquets* are manifold, and many of them are very ill.'

'What are we to do?' asked Bruna flatly. Her pale face and expressionless eyes had more effect on the old man than all the reproaches of the other pilgrims. Putting all the enthusiasm he could muster into his voice, he cried, 'Take heart, my friends! Take heart! Today we have scarce three more leagues to cover. We shall stop at Abrin. The Hospitalers of Saint John of Jerusalem have a commandership there, and we shall be taken in, I give you my word on it.'

'Hospitalers, fie!' said Ronan, not without anger. 'Let us hope they will earn their name by providing a good bed and hearty bowl of soup for these poor wandering souls, what say you, my friends?'

No one answered. The travellers had gone back to devouring their bread. They were waiting to set off again and did not dare remove their boots for fear that they would not be able to put them back on again, so painful and swollen were their feet.

'Come, Garin!' Humbert said. 'I should like to show you something.'

The young man rose and followed the old *Jacquet* to the town's ramparts.

'What do you see, my son?'

The young man hesitated for a moment and then said, 'Woods, hills, villages and . . . big clouds.'

'Look at those clouds well,' the old man said, pointing his iron staff to the horizon.

'They're . . . but, my God, Humbert, they be mountains! Are they our mountains?'

'Why yes, my boy, our Pyrenees, covered in snow. And behind them lies Galicia and Compostela! We are drawing close, Garin, drawing close!' the old man said, clapping him on the shoulder affectionately. But Garin did not even notice, he could not take his eyes from the blue-tipped peaks in the distance which he had mistaken for clouds.

55

Perched on a rocky ledge, the 'Commanderie' of Abrin looked like a fort. It was ringed by a thick stone wall above which the pilgrims' lanterns brightly shone. When they arrived the cart gate stood wide open and the friar porter, wearing his long white robe with the Hospitalers black cross, greeted them, 'God bless you, my brothers.'

'God bless you, Father,' replied Humbert. 'We are travelling to Compostela and would like to call on your hospitality.'

'And you shall be granted it with open arms, my brother. Come in, come in! How many are you?'

'We are eleven, Father. Three of our number are women, and one of them is sore unwell,' said Humbert, indicating Bérengère as she lay motionless on her stretcher.

The monk came over and nodded to show his concern.

'You are right, this poor woman is at the end of her strength. Come brothers, let us not stay out here!' said the monk, leading them into the courtyard. 'I shall take you to the hospice and I shall alert the friar nurse straight away. This is our chapel, should you wish to visit it,' added the monk, pointing out the small grey-stone building in front of them.

'Does it remain lit all the time?' asked Galeran, nodding towards the lantern that hung in a recess next to the chapel's porch.

'Night and day, my son,' replied the monk. 'The lantern

guides the pilgrims, and reminds us not only of our vocation but also, if need be, of God's presence in this place.'

A building the size of a tithe barn stood next to the chapel; it was the hospice. The monk stood aside to let them file into the vast room which contained some thirty cots. Some were separated from the others by makeshift curtains made of sheeting. The flagstone floor was covered with fresh brushwood, and there were thick woollen blankets neatly folded on each cot.

A novice ran over to them and greeted them. The monk sent him to find the friar nurse immediately.

'As you can see, this is our dorter. We have only one room, but it nevertheless allows us to welcome a good many pilgrims. Come this way,' the monk said to Guillaume and his son. 'Put this poor woman on this bed beside the brazier. She will be warm here.'

The straw mattress was new and apparently quite free of the fleas and mites that so often swarmed in the dorters used by *Jacquets*. The two men did as they were bidden in silence. Bérengère was soaked in sweat. She had not regained consciousness since they had left Lectoure.

'The two other women may take cots up at the end, we will curtain them off with sheets. Alas, we do not have a separate room for women pilgrims, they are so rare on Saint Jacques' route.'

'How can we thank you, Father?' said Humbert with a little bow. 'But I see that you already have some ten pilgrims with you,' he added.

'Why yes, and four more in the frater.'

Humbert's little group stood in the middle of the vast hall, dazed with exhaustion. The chevalier came up to the monk and said, 'God bless you for your hospitality, Father. You see the state we are in, might you have somewhere that we could wash ourselves?'

183

'It goes without saying, my son, I was about to suggest it to you. Here in Abrin we even have steam rooms and soap that we make ourselves. Put your belongings down on your cots and let those who wish to wash now follow me. I heard the blast of water earlier, the steam rooms must be ready.'

'Father,' interjected Bruna, 'we too should dearly like to wash. How will this be possible for my companion and myself?'

'Uhh,' said the monk, blushing as he contemplated the problem, 'I had not thought of this but . . . I shall send old Berthe to you, she is our cook. She will take you to her cell and prepare a tub of good hot water for you and something to dry yourselves.'

Bruna could not help smiling in the face of the monk's confusion.

He continued to address them all, saying 'As for your dirty clothes, a novice will come and take them shortly. You shall be given clean shifts when you have bathed. The bell will let you know when it is time to eat and time for Mass.'

Humbert heaved a contented sigh and said, 'Paradise, Father! Without blaspheming, I can say you are opening the doors of Paradise to us, and we sorely need it!'

56

The steam room at the 'Commanderie' of Abrin was in fact a tiny windowless room, filled with such thick steam that once inside, a man could scarcely see his own feet. The Hospitalers had set up two oak vats on a raised brick platform, and under this platform glowed hot coals. The water in the vats was very warm, and let off a lovely smell of thyme and lavender.

There were benches along the corridor, and a barber offered to shave them while they waited their turn for the bath.

'Here, have this, my son,' said the monk who attended the steam room, handing them two blocks of tallow soap. 'Pass them on to those after you when you come out. And here are some clean towels.'

Guillaume and Garin went into the steam room first, and the other pilgrims followed them, two by two.

When the chevalier went into the room with his brother, it occurred to him that they had not even spoken since Conques. Without a word they let their clothes fall to the floor and leapt into the fragrant water. Steam rose up around them forming a warm, damp screen. They stayed there like that for a long time before rousing themselves to wash, each scrubbing his tired, aching body vigorously.

Ronan came out first, stepping over the side of the tub and jumping fluidly to the ground. The chevalier could not help noticing the manifold scars on his elder brother's well-muscled body.

'Upon my word, Ronan, for a troubadour, you have more scars than an old boar!'

The *trouveur* turned towards him, his face distorted by a bitter sneer and he spat out these words, 'What sort of life do you think a troubadour leads then, little brother? A life full of women and money, rich with wealthy patrons and silk sheets? Fie, be done with all of that, I shall tell you what our life is made of! It is made of petty squabbles and sour wine, of snatched meals and plunderings, and of the girls that other men have cast aside.

The troubadour fell silent. The chevalier had climbed out of the bath and wrapped himself in a towel. He stood silent and motionless beside his brother.

'And you, the valiant knight,' Ronan whispered after a pause,

185

'do you know how a troubadour's life ends? While the poor fool is still dreaming of lying in the arms of some high-born lady, he ends up as carrion in the streets with a dagger in his back, or on the gallows to provide a feast for the crows, the rooks and the jackdaws!'

'Why do you not come back to Lesneven, Ronan?' breathed Galeran.

Ronan burst into a forced laugh and slapped Galeran's shoulder.

'Oh, little brother, you have not changed. But do you honestly believe that I, the eldest in line, I, Ronan de Lesneven, want pity from my own family?' Then he added more light-heartedly, 'Come, let us talk of nicer things and join our companions. I am so hungry I could eat a horse, and I really mean that!'

Galeran nodded, put on the long shift leant to him by the monks, and followed him without a word.

57

That night, despite the fact that he was so tired, the chevalier slept badly. He turned over and over on his cot, seeing his brother's features melting into those of the Moor woman with her tragic expression, haunted by the tortured bodies of innocent young men, and the white path flowing with blood which he could not stop.

With his arm folded under his neck, he lay watching the dancing flames of the *lucubrum*, a tiny lamp made of just a snippet of tow swimming in wax. Apart from the occasional loud snore and hoarse cough, nothing disturbed the silence in the dorter.

From where he lay he could see the whole room except for the area where the women were sleeping behind the curtain of sheeting. The only person who was not sleeping was Arastaigne who sat on his bed with his arms round his knees.

Galeran eventually fell asleep, then was woken by someone moaning; he heard the friar nurse rushing behind the makeshift curtain and glimpsed Bérengère writhing and arching her body. The poor woman was dying.

The chevalier sat on the edge of his bed and looked about him. Garin had been keeping watch over his mother but had fallen asleep on his cot. Galeran put on his boots hastily and went over to him, touching his shoulder gently. The poor boy woke with a start and looked at him blearily.

'It is I, Galeran. Come—' The chevalier could not finish his sentence before the boy was on his feet and running to his mother's side.

After administering the last rites, the friar nurse had come to stand beside Guillaume. The mason's face was grey with grief, he could not tear his eyes from his wife's tortured body, and did not even look up when his son fell to his knees beside him.

And that strange, wavering hour fell upon them: the hour when night dies away and dawn has not yet broken. Bérengère let out a little cry before grasping her husband's hand one last time and dropping back onto the bed, lifeless.

The chevalier made the sign of the cross. The curtain beside him was lifted and the old *Jacquet* came through and put his hand on Garin's shoulder. The boy was wracked with sobs.

58

After a brief funeral Mass, Bérengère's body was committed to the holy ground beside the little chapel of Abrin, where many *Jacquets*, killed by their arduous journey, already lay.

Guillaume, who had promised his wife that he would never leave her, decided to stay at the 'Commanderie' and offer his services to the monks. They accepted gratefully, only too pleased to have a mason in their midst. The poor man bid farewell to his travelling companions, held his son briefly to his breast and went back into the chapel. He no longer belonged to the outside world.

Humbert took Garin to one side and asked him what he wanted to do. The young man looked up at him with reddened eyes and spoke through the agonising constriction in his throat, 'To go on, Humbert, to go on!'

He could say no more than this, so great was his sorrow. The old *Jacquet* put his arm round the boy's shoulders and announced bracingly, 'We shall go and eat in the frater and then we shall leave, my boy. The white path and Bonaerges await us!'

Garin nodded and followed him towards the door of the hospice, where the others stood in a silent, forlorn little group.

59

The friar Hospitalers had not only prepared a good square meal for them, but had also laid out provisions for them to take in their travelling bags. A young novice stood by the great fireplace, watching over a pot blackened by the flames. He filled their bowls with a fine-smelling soup dotted with cloves of garlic and threads of cooked egg.

The pilgrims sat alongside each other on the benches, helping themselves to hunks of bread and cheese and wine from the carafes that the monks had set out along the table. Galeran nodded to his companions and went and sat down opposite Arastaigne on the other side of the frater. While he had lain awake the night before, he had come to understand the cleric's behaviour.

The murmur of general conversation and the occasional more boisterous outbursts from Manier and Ronan rang out under the vaulted stone ceiling. As he ate, the chevalier watched the cleric's thin face and noticed the dull, lifeless expression he wore.

Eventually, he made up his mind to speak and asked him calmly, 'To what order do you belong, Arastaigne?'

The cleric dropped his bowl which bounced off the bench and shattered on the floor. Suddenly the whole frater fell silent, and the travellers turned to look at the two men. The cleric hurriedly picked up the fragments of his bowl, and conversation started up again around the room.

Arastaigne stood bolt upright with the remains of his bowl in his hand. He was very pale and turned to the chevalier with a stunned expression.

'What . . . what do you mean, my lord?'

'I simply mean: to what order do you belong, Arastaigne?'

The man swallowed hard, his Adam's apple rising slowly back up his thin neck. With trembling fingers he put the broken pieces onto the table and fell heavily down onto the bench.

'How did you guess?'

'The way you move, the things you do, Arastaigne. The way you carry your hands joined, you walk barefoot; the fact that you wear a hood and the way you knot the rope around your waist . . . and the other night I saw what book it is that you read so fervently, the book you do not wish to share with anyone.'

'But you could not! I never leave it for a moment!' cried the cleric.

'Except to go to the steam room yesterday. Oh yes, you even hesitated to bathe yourself, parchment and steam are hardly happy bedfellows! But Manier persuaded you, and you left your bag on the bench.'

'That does not mean—'

'Indeed not! What could be more normal than for one of God's wanderers to have an illuminated manuscript! And especially one with illuminations that would not disgrace the library of a large abbey. The large abbey, in fact, whose seal it still bears.'

The man paled visibly.

'A manuscript whose very ink, whose ancient style of writing and whose Celtic designs bear witness to its great age and its origins in an English . . . or Irish scriptorium. Am I not right?'

The cleric remained speechless, as if stupefied by the chevalier's words.

'And the text,' went on the chevalier, 'more than anything,

the choice of text! The Book of Job, a book so permeated by despair . . .'

Arastaigne flushed and whispered, 'What do you want of me, Chevalier?'

'To know with whom I am dealing, that is all. I give you my word. There is no ill intent in my curiosity.'

The chevalier's frank expression seemed to convince Arastaigne. He nodded and started to speak slowly at first, and then increasingly quickly. It was as if this very singular man's defences had suddenly broken down and that this confession was providing him with instant relief.

'When my wife and only child died at the hands of thieves, I gave myself to God and entered the abbey in Bangor.'

'The abbey of Saint Columbus in Ireland?'

'Yes, my lord. My wife was from County Down, and it was as if I were going home to her. Bangor was taken over by Cistercians some five years ago, thanks to Malachie, the Bishop of Armagh, who was a great friend of Bernard de Clairvaux. Then . . .'

'Go on, Arastaigne,' encouraged the chevalier.

'Then . . . I failed. I could not pray to God. The more time passed the more I rebelled against Him. Every service became a torture of pretence. I resented Him for what He had done to me, what He had taken from me . . . I started to hate Him, may He forgive me for it now . . . There was only this one sacred book which really spoke to me. One night I fled, taking with me this book which I had stolen from the library.'

'And then?'

'Then I wandered aimlessly like a beggar. I spent two years like that until the day that I met a former *Jacquet*, a holy man who lived as a hermit in the Velay mountains. Something was reborn in me, not hope, oh no, just a glimmer of something, and I decided to make this pilgrimage. That is all.'

The chevalier remained silent for a moment, staring at the

191

cleric's hands which lay joined as if in prayer. Then he said, 'Arastaigne, how long have you been travelling with the young shepherd, Manier?'

The cleric looked up with a start.

'Why do you ask me that?'

'Answer me.'

'Well . . . we met in Le Puy. It was he who tagged along with me and I did not dare to turn him away. I seemed to amuse him and, when we were alone, he asked me manifold questions about the Bible. Then he disappeared and I did not see him until Aumont, no . . . Marchastel, I think. It was before joining Humbert and his group.'

'Thank you, Arastaigne, and may God keep you.'

'You will not betray me?'

The chevalier smiled.

'I give you my word, Arastaigne.'

60

Nine days later, in mid-May, the travellers reached the meeting of three ways in the midst of Basque country. Since leaving the rich lands of Gascony, they had crossed wild and wooded country, peopled by peasants whose guttural dialect was only comprehensible to Humbert and Manier. Even the crosses that stood all along their route bore inscriptions and symbols they could not decipher.

At this crossroads the *Jacquets* travelling from Tours, Vézelay and Le Puy all met. Hundreds of them converged on this place to proceed together to the ramparts of the great Basque city of Ostabat.

61

It was the quiet hour in the fortified city, that hour when merchants and peasants met in taverns, chatted on doorsteps and hailed the occasional brazen young damsel showing off her petticoats as she walked through the square.

The old archer was leaning against a narrow window, slowly emptying his fourth measure of diluted wine and thinking that if this waiting went on any longer he would end up a lowly drunkard . . . when he suddenly dropped his goblet, swearing as he did so, onto the sandy floor of the inn. He had just seen the chevalier walking past outside with his travelling companions.

Having tossed a few coins to the innkeeper, Jaufré hurried out of the inn and set off in pursuit of the pilgrims. When he caught up with them, he slowed his pace and mingled with the crowd, hiding each time the little group stopped and asked for bed and board for the night.

They eventually went into one of the Ospitalias and did not come back out again. After quite some time, the chevalier reappeared on the doorstep. He looked around indecisively. Then he heard two gentle whistling sounds coming from the next little street. The chevalier smiled and, without a moment's hesitation, set off down the alleyway.

The archer was waiting for him with a beaming face. Galeran greeted him warmly, only too happy to see him again.

'God bless you, my friend, what a pleasure to see you again.'

'Oh, my lord,' exclaimed the old man, 'I was beginning to despair! You certainly took a long time to get here. What can have happened to you?'

Galeran took him by the arm and, as they walked, he told him all the news: the goldsmith's death, the imprisonments in Cahors, the floods, Abrin and Bérengère . . . As he listened the old archer nodded in amazement and sympathy.

'But the goldsmith,' he said. 'His throat was cut cleanly, you say. The sergeant in Cahors must be right, he must have been killed by thieves like in Conques.'

'What do you mean like in Conques?' cried the chevalier.

'Oh yes, did I not tell you about it?' asked Jaufré.

'Explain yourself, Jaufré. When we met at Cahors you told me there had been no deaths along your route.'

'Indeed there were not, forsooth! Not any such as we were looking for, my lord. But on the day that you left Conques, I came across the men from the provost carrying a stretcher, bearing a man who had been carved up like a joint of meat.'

'Killed by knife wounds?'

'Most surely, my lord, nay even several wounds right in the heart! He was a nobleman. His clothes had not been taken, but there was not the tiniest piece of silver left on him.'

'Another one,' murmured the chevalier.

'But I thought . . .'

'The only thing we must think, my good Jaufré, is that we are leaving dead men in our wake!' replied the chevalier, as if closing the conversation.

The old archer coughed quietly before saying, 'I still have not seen the Baron de Peyre's messenger, Chevalier.'

'You shall stay here until he comes.'

'And you?'

'I shall go on as far as Roncevaux with them. The end is near, Jaufré, I am sure of it,' said the chevalier with determination.

'If the messenger arrives in time, I shall join you there, Chevalier. I have had my fill of drifting from one tavern to the next, it is no job for me.'

The chevalier's face brightened a little and he retorted, 'Indeed not, Jaufré! But take it from me and my recent experiences as a pilgrim, there is a great deal of good in horses and taverns!' And without another word the two men went their separate ways, keeping their concerns to themselves.

The pilgrims set off at first light. Before them stood the foothills of the great mountains that lay between them and Galicia.

62

The next day, having spent the night in a musty cow byre, they travelled through Saint-Jean-Pied-de-Port, passed under the vaulted doors of Notre-Dame and were preparing to cross the bridge over the Nive when they saw a group of self-appointed toll men waiting for them. There were three of them. Three strong men with hardened expressions and hefty clubs.

The chevalier, who was walking up ahead with Humbert, frowned anxiously. A few feet from the men, a pilgrim lay on the ground, with ripped clothes and blood on his face.

'Leave this to me, Chevalier,' whispered Humbert. 'I shall talk to them.'

Humbert greeted the toll men and started talking to them in the Basque language, which Galeran did not understand. The men watched him in silence but with hostility written all over their faces. Finally one of them shouted something at Humbert, and his words sliced through the air like a whip.

Humbert protested, shaking his head vigorously, showing them the shells on his mantle and indicating his humble companions. When he could get no further reaction from the toll men he turned to Galeran and said, 'These scoundrels are asking twelve *sous* for each of us when the toll is really less than four!'

'What would you like to do, Humbert, discuss it with them further?'

'Whatever happens, we cannot pay such a sum, so—'

'So, we go through!' said the chevalier jubilantly, bringing his hand to the hilt of his sword.

'We go through!' said Ronan who had come to stand beside him, and the three men bore down on the toll men who, realising that their luck was running dry, began to brandish their clubs and shriek threats. With one strong blow of his blade, the chevalier cut the first man's hand, and he dropped his club with a howl of pain. Galeran gave him a mighty kick which sent him rolling onto the bank where he lay motionless, bathed in his own blood.

'One down!' thought the chevalier, turning to his companions, only to realise with some regret that the whole matter was already settled. With one blow of his long iron staff the old *Jacquet* had well and truly knocked the second man unconscious at his feet. As for the third wastrel, Ronan had swiftly disarmed him and was holding him in an armlock.

He called to his brother, 'What shall we do with this rascal? I cannot listen to his squealing a moment longer!'

'First of all we give back whatever these good-for-nothings have taken from this poor old pilgrim, and with dividends, handsome dividends,' replied the chevalier, searching through the toll man's pockets.

The leather pouch he eventually found was bulging with coins. Galeran weighed it in his hand before helping the pilgrim to his feet and handing the entire pouch to him.

'With that, my friend, you can pay off several tolls and visit a fair few taverns to boot.'

The poor *Jacquet*, bemused by his change of fortune, sat down on a milestone, at a loss for words. Bruna went over to him and wiped his face gently to soothe him.

'Now what?' said Ronan, still holding his man who was foaming with rage.

'We knock him out and put him with his friends where they can try and extract a toll from the fish in the Nive!' replied the chevalier with a laugh.

63

A paved road wound up into the mountains and disappeared. According to Humbert, it was the old tin trail which led over the Pyrenean pass, the Port de la Cize as it was known locally. This was the road they would have to follow for some eight leagues before reaching Roncevaux.

Ronan launched into a hearty walking song, entreating his companions to join him. The little skirmish at the bridge had put them all in a joyful mood. Above them rose the mountains, so high that their peaks were swathed in cloud.

The pilgrims set off again with heavy feet. The higher they climbed the steeper became the incline. They soon left the old paved road for a grassy pathway which led to the top of the first slope.

'We're on a mountain called Leizar Atheka, and we shall soon be in Galicia,' said Humbert, leaning heavily on his iron staff while his fellow travellers fell to the ground on the wiry grass, and caught their breath.

'The sky's clouding over very quickly,' pointed out the chevalier, watching the horizon covered with scudding inky black clouds.

'Yes, you are quite right, my lord,' replied the old *Jacquet*. 'These mountains are similar in character to the ocean into which they fall. Their storms are just as terrible and destructive.' Then he turned to the travellers and called, 'Come on, my friends, we must set off, and don't drink so much, that is what makes your legs feel so heavy!'

Not one of them obeyed. The pilgrims were weary, and they sat staring mournfully at the ground, not moving a muscle.

'Hey, Humbert, a little peace, please! We have only just stopped and these confounded mountains are steeper than a bell tower!' exclaimed the blond shepherd.

'If you stay here, Manier, the storm will be after your skin.' Then Humbert added more firmly, 'Get up, my friends, we are nearing our goal. You will soon be in Roncevaux and we shall stay in the hostelry there for three days, so that we can build up our strength again. Come on, take heart, God's wanderers. Onwards and upwards!'

Bruna was the first to get stiffly to her feet, and she helped Lady Freissinge to stand up. Garin held out his hand to Manier. Ronan gave Master Raoul an encouraging pat on the shoulder to give him the courage to stand, and they set off again.

They made slow progress, leaning heavily on their pilgrims' staffs, keeping their eyes fixed on the ends of their boots or watching the pebbles rolling beneath their feet, and obstinately putting one foot in front of the other.

After some time of walking in silence like this, Manier tripped. He walked on with his eyes half closed, stumbled again and then rolled to the ground and immediately started to snore. Garin, who had been bringing up the rear with him, hurried over to him and tried in vain to wake him.

'Manier! Manier, wake up!' he cried.

The other man snored all the louder. Garin looked round. The others were disappearing behind a rise in the land. He turned back to his blond companion and slapped him. Manier opened his eyes immediately and stared at him strangely before grumbling sleepily, 'Hey, hey, enough! What are you hitting me for?'

'The others are going on ahead, Manier. Get up!'

'I'm getting up, give me your hand, my boy!' And, taking his outstretched hand, he got to his feet. He set off again slowly, walking hesitantly and occasionally clinging to the young man's mantle.

'Go a little faster, Manier. They're already a long way ahead, I can no longer see them.'

'Oh, I can't,' grumbled the other. 'Even if I wanted to, I couldn't. And, anyway, why don't you just leave me on my own then?'

Garin shook his head and resigned himself to walking at the same speed as the shepherd.

64

After going down the slope on the other side, the pilgrims followed a stony path towards an ancient wood of beech trees and sweet chestnuts. At least there they would be sheltered from the wind. Sometimes muttering a prayer, sometimes silent, they carried on until they reached a river source where Humbert raised his hand to bring them to a halt.

Bruna bent to pick up a little cross made of twigs bound together with a long blade of grass, then another and a third.

She picked up dozens of them and took them over to show Humbert.

'What are these, my lord?'

'They are offerings made by all those who have travelled before us, and there is still more in store to amaze you, Bruna. When we reach the cross of Charlemagne at the Port de la Cize, you too shall fashion a cross as is the custom, for that is what the great King Charles did long ago.'

'Humbert!' called Galeran with a note of anxiety in his voice. The old *Jacquet* turned to see the chevalier coming towards him.

'Where are Garin and Manier.'

Humbert looked round in alarm. The two young men were no longer with them.

'They were bringing up the rear,' he whispered.

'I saw Manier fall before we came into the woods,' said Bruna. 'Garin was trying to get him back on his feet. After that I didn't really see what happened.'

The chevalier's face had paled. He threw a glance at the old *Jacquet* who lowered his head.

'Go and find them, Chevalier. We shall wait for you here.' And when he looked up Galeran had already disappeared, swallowed up by the surrounding forest.

65

Despite Garin's protests, Manier had dropped to the ground on a mound of soft moss, grabbed his calabash and shaken it.

'Nothing left to drink,' he said with obvious disappointment.

Garin stood leaning against a tree, waiting. He threw him his own calabash impatiently.

'You would do better to obey Humbert instead of drinking so much water! And now, Manier, if you don't get back up, I'm leaving you here!'

The other man caught the calabash but dropped it as he tried to bring it to his lips.

'Oh, I'm so clumsy,' he cried.

'Indeed you are,' said Garin in exasperation.

'Listen!'

The young mason strained his ears, but could only hear the wind rustling in the boughs of the magnificent trees.

'What is it? I can hear nothing.'

'Are you deaf, then?' said Manier, getting to his feet. 'Come, there must be a stream nearby. I can hear running water. We can fill our calabashes.'

'I'm not thirsty, and are you sure you're not hearing things?'

'I heard it, I tell you. And Humbert told me there was a stream in the woods,' announced the other, heading off into a thicket. Garin sighed in exasperation and followed him despite himself, forgetting to pick up his staff as he set off. In a few strides he caught up with his companion who was still forging through the undergrowth.

'Wait for me!'

'We're nearly there, come on!' said Manier hurrying as if suddenly forgetting how tired he was. Scratched and snagged by low branches and brambles, Garin managed to plough his way through the thick scrub and eventually came out into a little clearing where the shepherd had come to a stop.

Manier was looking around with satisfaction. The bramble thickets formed an impenetrable rampart around them. Mossy rocks rose up out of the ground, but there was no sign of a stream. The middle of the clearing was dominated by the remains of an oak tree which had been struck by lightning, a great black carcass covered in lichen. Manier went over and sat down by it, and started rummaging through his bag.

'But,' said Garin in amazement, 'what are you doing now? You can see there is no stream here. Come on, we must go. We have lost enough time, the others will be worried. He turned on his heel, because he was now beginning to feel strangely anxious.

'You're right, my boy, we've wasted enough time!' Manier's voice sounded right by the young man's ear, startling him. The shepherd had jumped lithely to his feet and was now standing behind Garin with one hand on his shoulder.

'But what are you—' the young man started to protest, turning to the shepherd.

'Don't move or I'll cut you!' growled the other.

'You're mad!' cried Garin, feeling the blade of a knife at his throat.

'And you are as crafty as a naughty little childer, my boy! A childer who knows how to sing!'

'What do you mean?'

The other man gave no reply, he merely applied a little pressure with his knife to Garin's throat. Suddenly the young mason was frozen with fear: in a flash he saw the goldsmith's dead body in the ruins of the Roman theatre.

'Was it you who killed Master Pierre? Tell me. That's it isn't it? So you could steal his silver *markas*. But I don't have any money, so what do you want from me?'

'Well, if I'd known the old boy had so much money, I might well've taken him, but he wasn't my type, too old, too ugly. But you, on the other hand, you please me well, you know.'

'But you're talking nonsense, you were talking about wanting to marry some girl!'

'And you believed me, you poor fool!' said Manier with a mocking laugh.

202

'But you must be completely mad!' protested Garin, trying to free himself.

Manier became angry.

'Oh, no, my little one! Not twice in a row!' he cried, and he struck a heavy blow on the nape of Garin's neck, throwing him forward so that he fell flat on his face in the grass. The young shepherd laughed heartily. 'Now, that's better. You see, you'll have to learn to be quiet, my sweet. And now, leave this to me,' he whispered, leaning over the inanimate body.

Manier used his blade to cut through Garin's clothes so that he was soon naked. He leant over Garin and looked at him. Manier was humming to himself quietly, his knife raised, ready to strike. At that very moment a hand grabbed him by the neck and hauled him backwards. Manier let go of his knife and fell to the ground. Before him stood the chevalier, his face distorted with rage.

'So it was you!' he growled. 'I thought as much, but you almost stopped, you'd become cautious, had you not?'

Manier tried to get to his feet.

'Stay there!' Galeran ordered. 'Or in the name of God I shall run my sword through you; and I hope you realise that if this poor boy is dead you shall follow him without a doubt!'

Without taking his eyes off the shepherd, but still holding his sword in his hand, the chevalier went over to Garin. The rise and fall of his chest reassured him: the boy had only been knocked out. Galeran turned back to the shepherd, who had not moved. He was looking about him wildly as if looking for a means of escape.

'I will leave you no way out, Manier!' said the chevalier going over to the young man who scrambled to his feet.

'My lord, of what do you accuse me?' he sobbed. 'We had a fight, I was just checking that he wasn't dead!'

'What a pretty story!' sneered the chevalier. 'What you do not

203

know, Manier, is that I have been following you since Marchastel. And that I've watched every time boys like this one have been committed to the ground with a few wounds added and their lives taken away!'

The shepherd blanched, he was in tears, and he threw himself at Galeran's feet. The chevalier was overcome by an intense feeling of revulsion, and his knuckles whitened as they gripped his sword. The shepherd grovelled at his feet, raising his arms in supplication:

'In the name of almighty God, pity!'

Utterly disgusted, the chevalier stepped back instinctively, tripping on a stone and falling backwards. As if this was exactly what he had been waiting for, Manier reacted with astonishing speed. He grabbed his knife which had fallen to the ground and threw himself at Galeran, his blade raised at the ready.

The chevalier managed to catch hold of his arm, but his adversary seemed to be possessed of superhuman force. His eyes were demented, his mouth distorted with hatred, and the blade of his knife came inexorably closer to the chevalier's throat. Then suddenly a stunned expression flitted over the shepherd's face. His mouth slackened and a bloody dribble spewed from his lips. He dropped his knife and slumped forwards onto Galeran.

He was dead, a fine dagger had been driven into his back right up to the hilt.

'Not bad, would you not say, little brother?' said Ronan, stepping out of the thickets. 'I was afraid this wastrel would end up hacking you apart.'

Galeran fought his way free of the shepherd's bloodied body, and stood up. On the other side of the clearing, Garin was regaining consciousness and trying to sit up, astonished to find himself unharmed and quite naked.

'You saved my life, Ronan,' the chevalier said solemnly.

'Indeed, it would seem so,' the troubadour replied simply,

rummaging unashamedly through the shepherd's belongings. The chevalier came over, unable to take his eyes off his brother.

'Hey, look at this, little brother! He was not so poor after all,' he said, holding out a handful of gold and silver *deniers*.

66

When Jaufré met up with Galeran at Roncevaux three days later, the chevalier greeted him with a brief, 'It's over, Jaufré, the beast is dead, we've leaving!'

'But the messanger . . . he gave me this for you from the Baron de Peyre. Who was the beast then, my lord? Was it as terrifying as we believed?'

The chevalier took the parchment and put into his leather pouch, laughing.

'Oh no, my friend, the killer was as beautiful as a cherub, his golden hair was as curly as the fleeces of the sheep he said he tended.'

'So it was the shepherd Manier who was travelling in your group?' murmured the old archer thoughtfully.

'As you so rightly say. He was sly as a fox and more vicious than you could imagine. At the moment he is making his excuses to his own kind; cloven-hoofed demons,' said Galeran, going over to Quolibet.

The charger whinnied, pawed the ground and shook his long, shining mane.

'It does me good to see you again, my old Quolibet,' the chevalier whispered, stroking the animal's neck and muzzle before springing up into the saddle.

The archer frowned. There was something about the chevalier's attitude he really could not understand.

'Do you wish to leave straight away?' he asked. 'And your friends, your brother? Are we not to bid them farewell?'

'It is already done!' replied Galeran, kicking his charger into a trot in the great echoing courtyard of the hospice. Going through the cart gate, the chevalier launched his horse towards the Port de la Cize and towards France.

Watching him disappearing in the distance, Jaufré leapt quickly into his own saddle and with a lash of his whip, headed off after him.

Epilogue

The two men had parted ways at Conques and, while Jaufré travelled steadily back for the Baron de Peyre's lands, Galeran had suddenly decided to turn back towards Spain. He rode swiftly along the *camino francés* heading for Compostela.

He climbed over mountains, crossed the sierras, passed olive groves and negotiated ravines to reach Burgos in just four days, and there he stopped at the hospice of San-Juan Evangelista.

He arrived whitened from head to foot by the white dust of the roads. He led his horse slowly to the water trough and then to the stable, where he rubbed him down and gave him a deep bed of fresh straw, before collapsing fully dressed onto his own bed where he slept for two days, in the grip of fever and delirium from sunstroke.

Two days later he set off again, and three days after that he crossed the Roman bridge at Astorga and stopped for the night in the fortified town. The next day Quolibet was lame, so the chevalier led him gently to Compludo where the monks at San-Juan had told him there was a forge and a farrier.

The man beat out a new shoe and plunged the glowing iron into a trough of water before nailing it to Quolibet's hoof. Galeran paid him his due and set off again along the white path.

Four days later he was caught up in the midst of a long stream of pilgrims climbing the Monte del Gozo. He dismounted and joined them in their arduous climb.

When they reached the top, the *Jacquets* threw themselves to their knees in a divinely inspired trance. They wept, chanted and cried, 'Oh joy! Oh joy! Santiago!' Before them, scarcely half a league away, they could at last see the holy town of Santiago de Compostela, asylum for all God's wanderers.

It was mid-July and there had been a succession of ceremonies in honour of Saint Jacques since the beginning of the month, a month in which the pilgrims kept on arriving in their droves to pay homage to Bonaerges.

The chevalier went into the cathedral and, like so many of the exhausted pilgrims, he laid his hands on the marble pillar of the tree of Jesse. Then he ploughed through the crowds towards the crypt and the high altar, kissing it before going and kneeling to pray a little way away.

Suddenly a hand touched his shoulder gently, startling him.

'But, Chevalier, why are you here? I thought you had returned to your country.'

Galeran stood up. Arastaigne stood before him, but a quite different Arastaigne to the one he had last seen. He held himself upright and looked somehow relieved as if he were no longer suffering in the depths of his soul.

'Yes,' said Galeran, 'I went as far as Conques and then turned back. In fact, I am trying to find our travelling companions. Are they in Santiago?'

'Why no, Chevalier. Only Lady Freissinge, Raoul and myself. The other four have set off for Notre-Dame de Finibus Terrae!'

'Is Lady Freissinge no longer with young Bruna, then?'

'No, my lord,' replied Arastaigne. 'After she reached the cathedral here, she asked Humbert to take her to the new San-Lazaro hospice.'

'The lepers' hospice, the one they are still building along the route?'

'Yes, my lord. She asked that she might tend the most lowly, the most humble. I believe she has turned her back on her life in the outside world.'

Galeran nodded.

'And did Ronan the troubadour stay with the others?' he asked.

'I believe so.'

'Where is this Notre-Dame de Finibus Terrae?'

'From what Humbert told me, it is at the very ends of Galicia, just inland from the costa de La Muerte, at cabo Fisterra.'

The two men remained silent for a moment, then Galeran said gently, 'You have changed a great deal, Arastaigne.'

'Yes,' replied the other with no trace of pride. 'As you see, Saint Jacques does perform miracles. I shall return to Bangor, Chevalier, to give back that which I stole. And if my brothers will still have of me, I shall withdraw from the world, and for good this time!'

Having bid farewell to Arastaigne, Galeran mounted his charger again and headed for cabo Fisterra. He travelled over rocky crests and through ancient highland woods, before coming out beside the rias de Muros, a wide estuary flooded by the sea like those he knew in the Léon region.

This journey took Galeran into a landscape that seemed familiar to him although he had never seen it before. Worn, bare rocks, walls and houses of granite, slate roofs. He felt as if he were back home, at 'the end of the world' in his native Brittany. The sea air whipped his face and seagulls flew off with haunting, piercing cries. Quolibet whinnied with joy and set off at a trot along the coastal path which looked down on wild salt creeks.

At last Galeran saw the dark cliffs of cabo Fisterra less than a league away and he urged his charger forward. Soon all that lay between him and the ocean was the little chapel of Notre-Dame de Finibus Terrae, the sanctuary 'beyond which there is no ground beneath the feet'.

The place seemed to be deserted. The chevalier tied Quolibet up to an old tree stump and walked all the way round this coastal sanctuary, before stopping dead in his tracks.

Ronan was sitting in the doorway of the chapel, with two scallop shells on the ground in front of him.

He looked up to his younger brother and said calmly, 'I was waiting for you, little brother.' Then he burst out laughing and rose to his feet. 'Do not look at me like that! You see, I know how stubborn you are, I knew you would find me again. You could not let me go like that.'

With a sad smile playing on his lips, Galeran replied, 'You are right, I could not.'

Ronan took his brother by the arm and led him to the edge of the cliff.

'When I arrived here,' he said, 'I had a peculiar feeling of coming home. Look at the shallows, the reefs, the promontories . . . they call to mind any number of shipwrecks and mortal accidents. An ideal place for us to meet again, would you not say?'

The ocean lay at their feet, stretching as far as the eye could see. They stayed like that for a long time, side by side, in silence, more united than they had ever been. Then Ronan moved a few steps away, and the spell was broken. He announced dryly, 'I'm listening now.'

The chevalier's face darkened, and he spoke in a sad, gloomy voice that was far from his usual incisive tones, 'For me, it all started in Vézelay with a prediction from a Moor woman. And then there were those poor youngsters assassinated in such monstrous fashion, and I set off following the *Jacquets* and your little group. Then I met up with you in Conques. You, the eldest in line, the proud Ronan de Lesneven, you were stooping to pick up paltry coins in front of the abbey. You tried your best to avoid me. You were in turn jubilant and inconsolably sad, like that time in the steam room at Abrin.' The chevalier paused before continuing, 'Since we left Aubrac, the man I was following had stopped killing, or had somehow been hindered. I understood why later. But it was when I came to look at Master Pierre's body that I thought that there were probably two killers, not one!'

Ronan had turned pale, and could not take his eyes off his brother.

'There had already been a murder in Le Puy, another at Conques, and then in Cahors . . . I did not believe for one moment in the story about brigands, but, on the goldsmith's body, I saw the characteristic marks left by a man of arms and bloodshed. These murders were not like the others, they were efficient, carried out quickly, and they were committed for the victim's money, because all these victims were rich and carrying money on them.'

'But you must have seen that the little shepherd had money on him?' Ronan spat out in spite of himself.

'Money that you very quickly slipped into your own pocket, my brother. Because the second murderer was none other than you!'

Ronan made no protest. He had gone back to sit down in the doorway to the humble little chapel.

'You see, what confused me,' went on Galeran, 'was Lady Freissinge! She was most unusual, this woman so closely guarded by Bruna. In fact, from what you say, the girl watched over her even more closely after Conques. Now, what was it that happened there? A rich gentleman was stabbed to death in the street. So, for a while, I thought that Lady Freissinge and the assassin were one and the same. But then, in Cahors, she did not leave Bruna and Humbert. I checked. Only, I admit, I needed the report from the Baron de Peyre to understand who Bruna and Lady Freissinge really were.'

Ronan looked up.

211

'I do not know that myself,' he murmured.

'Lady Freissinge was a beautiful woman,' went on Galeran, 'perhaps too beautiful, and indeed too weak to be the wife of one man alone. She loved to be loved, and she could not control her desire, giving herself to all and sundry. Her husband, Lord d'Apchon, came across her one day in the arms of one of her lovers. He had the man seized by his guards, and cleaved the man's chest in two with one blow of his axe, tore out his heart and threw it at Lady Freissinge's feet. He wanted to kill her, but he could not do it because his own heart still belonged to this woman even though she had continually betrayed him. So he decided to exile her by sending her to Compostela and, to ensure that she did come back alive, he entrusted her to the care of a mere girl – a girl whose upright character he knew but whose strength and courage he could not have guessed – damsel Bruna.'

After a long silence, Ronan eventually said quietly, 'It was in Le Puy that I met her, in the back streets, and I realised she could be useful to me. Even though she had strayed from a life of righteousness, perhaps because of that, she was so powerfully seductive that men were fascinated by her.'

'And you, you waited for these lovestruck fools to sneak up and rob them: you used her as bait!' exclaimed Galeran.

'Bruna may have realised what I was doing,' went on Ronan. 'In any event, she no longer let her mistress out of her sight, and now her mistress will charm only the most hideous lepers.'

The troubadour stood up and went over to his brother, putting a hand on his shoulder.

'If you knew I was guilty, little brother, why did you not hand me over to the justice system?'

'Please stop calling me little brother!' replied the chevalier, shaking himself free angrily. 'And if you thought that I had

212

worked out your little game, why did you not let Manier finish off the task in that clearing at Roncevaux?'

'Fie, I cared little for that golden-haired shepherd!' cried Ronan. 'And now you have caught up with me. Why?'

'There was a mention, in the baron's note, of one Ronan de Bretagne who wielded the rebec as ably as he did the blade, a troubadour whom many a provost was trying to catch to take him to the gallows!'

'Fie, if it were just the provosts!' Ronan sighed. 'I set off for the Orient, like so many others, to find fortune and honour, or to die there. Instead of that I fell in with cruel ruffians who wanted to kill me when I left them. As I fled from them, I lost my one and only friend, they slit his throat instead of mine on a terrace in Tripoli . . . So I returned to Paris and I lost what little I had at cards and at chess. Then I did every lowly thing that can be done in the streets after the curfew, with the vagabonds and the street girls . . . both of whom empty your pockets in their own way! What difference does stealing and killing make in that sort of world?' The troubador's voice faltered. He looked out to sea and remained silent for a long time. 'And, Galeran, even though it may be too late, I repent of all these misdeeds now.'

'Where will you go, Ronan?' replied the chevalier simply.

The troubadour gave a sort of groan. 'Are you then leaving me free to go?'

'You are in God's hands.' The chevalier sighed. 'Humbert once told me that he believed in redemption.' Galeran in turn remained silent for a moment. 'But,' he added in a lighter tone, 'what actually happened to our master *Jacquet*?'

The troubadour shrugged.

'Believe me if you will. Humbert, after just one day's rest, was quite restored and already talking about travelling home!'

'And Bruna and the young mason? Did they get to the very end?'

'Now, when it comes to getting to the end, they certainly got to the very end!' said the troubadour, sitting up and pointing. 'Can't you see them, over there on the shore?'

The chevalier risked a quick glimpse over the scrub along the cliff's edge, the gnarled branches forming a sort of balcony over the void. He saw the vast expanse of the sea and down on the beach two little figures walking arm in arm, perfectly in step, along the edge of the waves.

'There!' sighed Ronan, 'my Queen of Sheba gave up her heart to that young whippersnapper Garin . . .'

'Don't tell me you're jealous, Ronan!'

'Forsooth no!' retorted the troubadour bitterly. 'I've known for a long time that youth belongs with youth, and that God and women prefer the young . . . little brother!'

May this be the end of the book
But not the end of the journey

Bernard de Clairvaux

Author's Note

More than eight centuries have passed since these events, and still thousands of people follow in the footsteps of the twelfth century *Jacquets*, crossing rivers, climbing hills and mountains, braving rain and snow, to reach Santiago de Compostela.

Notre-Dame in Le Puy, Saint-Michel in Aiguilhe, the Dômerie in Aubrac, Conques, Moissac, Lectoure, Abrin, Roncevaux, and many other places besides, are still the stages along the white path which takes these pilgrims to 'the end of the earth'.

Mediaeval Recipes
from the Time of
Chaevalier de Lesneven

Just as in our country the wind brings down leaves and twigs
... in the Orient it brings the smell of spices down from the
trees of Paradise ...

In mediaeval times these same spices were everywhere: at the
banquets of the nobility; on finely decked merchants' tables;
and even on the more frugal tables of an abbey. In the Middle
Ages meats and pastries were paired up with milk of almonds,
honey, cloves, cinnamon, nutmeg, ginger, galangal, cardamom,
saffron, mace, zedoary – otherwise known as the grains of
paradise!

So precious were these spices that it was believed that
cinnamon came from phoenix nests and that peppercorns
were protected by serpents which had to be burned to death
before anyone could harvest the flame-blackened pepper!

In the Middle Ages eating spices was to dream, to be in heaven
on earth!

Fiery Sauce

6 eggs
5 dessertspoons olive oil
2 small chilli peppers

saffron
salt and freshly ground pepper
3 teaspoons vinegar

- Hard boil the eggs.
- Mash the six cooked yolks and moisten with the olive oil.
- Add the crushed chillies, saffron, salt pepper and vinegar.
- Blend to a smooth paste.

Serve this sauce with cold meats to set your guests' palates alight.

Lamb Parcels with Eau-de-Vie

500g leg of lamb cut into 6 chunks
6 thin slices of smoked bacon
olive oil
salt and pepper to taste
thyme, laurel, cloves
½ litre eau-de-vie
chanterelles (or other mushrooms if they are not available)
chestnuts, cooked and peeled
juice of one lemon (optional)

- Wrap each chunk of lamb in a slice of bacon and tie it up with string.
- Heat the oil in a heavy based frying pan with salt, pepper and herbs, and brown the parcels.
- When the pan is really hot pour in the eau-de-vie and set it alight.
- Shake the pan until the flames have gone out.
- Add the mushrooms and chestnuts and cook over a moderate heat until the lamb is done to your liking.
- Lay out the parcels on a serving dish.

- Reduce the sauce slightly (adding the lemon juice if desired) and serve in a sauceboat.

Almond Milk

200g of unpeeled almonds
$\frac{1}{2}$ litre milk or water
2 slices of stale white bread, made into breadcrumbs

- Soak the almonds for twenty-four hours before peeling them.
- Mash them with a pestle and mortar or in a blender.
- Heat, with the milk or water and the breadcrumbs, for a few minutes.
- Pass through a fine sieve.

Almond milk can be salted or sweetened, depending on the recipe.

Cream of Mixed Nuts

This recipe serves six, and the consistency can be changed to suit your taste by lengthening the cooking time.

140g mixed ground almonds, walnuts and hazelnuts
$\frac{1}{2}$ litre of almond milk (see previous recipe)
spiced honey (see following recipe)

- Blend the ground nuts with the almond milk.
- Heat gently and stir until thickened.
- Pour the cream into a soufflé dish or into individual ramekins and leave to cool.
- Drizzle with spiced honey before serving.

Spiced Honey

3 tablespoons acacia honey
1 dessertspoon grated lemon zest
1 dessertspoon powdered cinnamon
1 dessertspoon grated fresh ginger

- Mix all the ingredients together well for a fragrant spicy addition to many desserts.

Bon appétit!

Glossary of Mediaeval Terms

Aquamanile: a water carrier made from a pig or sheep's bladder or from a gourd.

Bailiff: a feudal lord's overseer, usually his closest, most trusted servant.

Ballock dagger: a small dagger with two small balls (ballockys) at the end of the handle to stop the user's hand slipping onto the blade.

Calabash: a water container made of a hollowed-out gourd.

Camino francés: the Spanish name given to the route taken by the French pilgrims.

Caparison: a decorated hood or other covering for a horse.

Capuchon: a hooded cape.

Chasuble: a long, sleeveless over-garment worn by priests during Mass.

Childer, childling: colloquial terms for young children.

Coney: a rabbit.

Cot: a common mediaeval word for a simple bed which may have constituted just a straw mattress, or may have had a simple wooden frame.

Dômerie: a fortified monastery.

Dorter: a dormitory for several people in a monastery or convent.

Doublet: a fitted waist- or hip-length tunic usually made of wool, worn by men throughout the Middle Ages.

Fletchings: the feathers on arrows.

Frankish: relating to the Franks, the forerunners of the modern French people.

Frater: the dining room or refectory in a monastery or convent.

Galicia: ancient name for the region of north-west Spain on the Bay of Biscay.

Hauberk: a mail shirt worn by knights.

Head-wrap: a simple white linen bonnet.

Hose: finely knitted garments worn on the legs, forerunners of tights, socks and stockings.

Infidels: those who did not have faith in the Christian God, from the Latin for faithless.

Kirtle: a dress of linen or wool.

Lavatorium: an area in a monastery or convent used for washing.

League: an ancient unit of distance approximately equal to two kilometres.

Madder: the red-purple colour obtained from the root of the yellow-flowered madder plant.

Mantilla: a scarf of lace or silk worn over a woman's head.

Mantle: a coat or cape, often of wool or leather.

Mesne: the parts of an estate that were worked by tenant farmers known as villeins.

Paladin: one of the twelve peers of the legendary King Charlemagne's court, or any knight believed to equal them in courage and valour.

Palfrey: a docile riding horse.

Pillory: a wooden frame, sometimes shaped like a wheel, to which offenders were attached and then left to the mercy of the crowd.

Postern: a back door or secondary entrance.

Provost: a figure of authority, usually with legal powers, in a large estate or an entire community.

Quatrain: a four-line poem or a poem made up of four-line verses, usually with alternate rhymes.

Rebec: a stringed instrument, a forebear of the modern violin.

Sanatorium: a place of medical care and healing, like a modern hospital.

Saponin: a foaming steroid found in a particular group of plants and used to make soaps and detergents.

Scriptorium: a place where books and documents were stored and copied.

Shift: a white linen undershirt.

Strop: a leather strap used for sharpening the blade of a razor.

Surcoat: an outer garment made of wool or leather, sometimes with fur trimmings.

Tallow: a fatty substance rendered from the suet of sheep and cattle and used in foods as well as in candle- and soap-making.

Troubadour: a singer or lyric poet, also known in mediaeval France as a *trouveur*.

Vassal: a holder of land by feudal tenure on conditions of homage and allegiance to his lord.

Vellum: fine parchment made from calf or pig skin.

Wax tablet and stylus: a tablet of wood coated in wax and a sharp instrument made of wood, bone or metal were used throughout the Middle Ages, especially for communication between monks observing the rule of silence.

The Mediaeval Monastic Timetable

Nocturns: Mass held towards 2 o'clock in the morning.

Matins: Mass held just before dawn.

Prime: Mass held at about 7 o'clock in the morning.

Terce: Mass held at about 9 o'clock in the morning.

Morrow Mass: held in the middle of the morning.

Sexte: the sixth Mass of the day, held at midday.

None: Mass held at 2 o'clock in the afternoon.

Vespers: from the Latin word, *vespera*, evening. Mass held at about 5 o'clock in the afternoon.

Compline: Mass held at about 8 o'clock in the evening.

Prominent Figures in Twelfth-Century France

Abelard: (1070–1142) Philosopher, theologian and dialectician. He founded the Abbey of Paraclet where Eloise became abbess. Bernard de Clairvaux obtained his condemnation at the Council of Sens in 1140.

Eleanor of Aquitaine: (1122–1204) After her divorce from Louis VII in 1152 she married Henry Plantagenet in the same year and bore him several children (most notably Richard the Lionheart). She ended her days in the abbey at Fontevrault, where she is buried.

Louis VII: (1120–1180) King of France, crowned in Reims on 25 October 1131. In 1137 he married Eleanor of Aquitaine. He participated in the second Crusade with Conrad III. He was divorced in 1152 and married Constance de Castille. After her death, he married Adèle de Champagne, mother of Philippe II Auguste. He died on 18 September 1180.

Bernard de Clairvaux: (1091–1153) Having taken holy orders in Cîteaux in 1112, he became the first Abbot of Clairvaux in 1115. At Vézelay, in 1146, he was a great advocate of the second Crusade. He argued against the *Ordre de Cluny*.

Suger: (1081–1151) Monk and politician. He became Abbot of Saint-Denis in 1122 and was a friend and fellow student of

Louis VI. He acted as an adviser to Louis VII and was regent to the kingdom of France during the second crusade.

Pierre III: Bishop of Le Puy Sainte-Marie from 1145 to 1155.

Adalard, Viscount of Flanders: A descendant of Baudoin I, Adalard founded the Dômerie at Aubrac and died on 5 May 1135. His successor was Guiral who was himself succeeded by his brother Etienne.

Abbot Géraud: Abbot of Moissac from 1140 to 1150.